CW01433024

BODY AT THE DOCTOR'S

A gripping British crime thriller

DIANE M. DICKSON

THE
BOOK
FOLKS

The Books Folks
A Joffe Books Company
www.thebookfolks.com

First published in Great Britain in 2025

© Diane M. Dickson 2025

This book is a work of fiction. Names, characters, businesses, organizations, places and events are either the product of the author's imagination or are used fictitiously. Any resemblance to actual persons, living or dead, events or locales is entirely coincidental. The spelling used is British English except where fidelity to the author's rendering of accent or dialect supersedes this. The right of Diane M. Dickson to be identified as author of this work has been asserted in accordance with the Copyright, Designs and Patents Act 1988.

No part of this book may be used or reproduced in any manner for the purpose of training artificial intelligence technologies or systems. In accordance with Article 4(3) of the Digital Single Market Directive 2019/790, Joffe Books expressly reserves this work from the text and data mining exception.

BODY AT THE DOCTOR'S *is the ninth title
in the Detective Jordan Carr mystery series.*

A list of characters can be found at the back of this book.

Chapter 1

Detective Inspector Jordan Carr didn't need anyone telling him which way to go. He could smell the blood.

He was careful to stay on the plastic stepping plates of the safe route. His scene suit pulled and pinched his shoulders and arms. One-size-fits-nobody was the usual complaint. He had dragged on the flimsy garment and grabbed some shoe covers while standing at the rear of the SOC van parked on double yellow lines in Rodney Street.

Jordan gave his name to the bobby on duty, flashed his warrant card, signed the clipboard, and then passed through the large double doors into the grand building.

He followed the cloying odour to the first-floor landing, where the crime scene manager Sergeant Ted Bliss turned to look at him and raised a thumb in acknowledgement.

"Dr Jasper is attending," Ted said. "He hasn't come far. He was already at the city morgue, so just around the corner. Sergeant Vickie Frost is leading the SOC team. She's with him at the mo. The gang's all here. How come you picked this one up, though?"

Jordan shrugged his shoulders. "Not sure, to be honest. Possibly staff shortages in St Anne Street and my DCI thought I had nothing better to do."

"Aye well, when you've been behind a desk in Copy Lane as long as DCI Lewis, I reckon you lose touch. Are you bringing your own team?"

"Stella's on her way."

"DC Grice?" Ted asked. "He's usually with you, isn't he?"

"We'll see. John's got his hands full at the moment."

"Haven't we all, mate? Anyway, I'll let you get on."

Jordan turned a full circle. The blood was everywhere. Smeared on the door frame and spattered across the fine wood panelling. It was pooled on the carpet, thick and dark, and trailed in footprints towards a fire door at the rear of the landing.

Lying across the entrance to a large, bright room was the bulky body of a man. He was late middle age, dressed in a navy suit that had been stained with gore. His clothes were slashed and dishevelled by whatever had happened. His thick grey hair was glued into spikes and clumps by the blood. He was obviously dead.

Dr James Jasper, the chief Liverpool medical examiner, turned to nod at Jordan. "Good to see you, Carr. I still have a little more to do here and then we'll be taking this chap to my morgue. We know who he is already. This is his consulting room. Mr Roland Vance. Surgeon. Don't know him myself, thank heavens. But he qualified about the same time as I did, but down in London, according to the certificates on his wall."

Jordan glanced around again. There was little he could do here and would only be in the way if he stayed. Everything was being photographed and videoed, and there would be an opportunity later, after the fingertip searches and sample-harvesting, for him to have access.

"Any idea when you'll be doing the examination?"

"Huh, usual bloody question," Jasper growled. "I might get to it today, I might not. If I don't, it will be next week. Mrs Jasper and I are going to the cottage in Wales for a few days to say goodbye to the summer, and it is not optional. Her sister is already there and the car's packed. So, you'll have to hope things go smoothly with my other cases today. I'll let you know." With that, he turned back to his grisly work.

Jordan knew it was pushing his luck, but in for a penny and all that. "Any thoughts about time of death?" he said.

The look he was given could have soured milk, but it was followed by a quick twitch of the lips as Jasper raised his eyebrows.

"I'm not known to enjoy guessing games, Detective Inspector. However, if you bothered to look, his tie is loosened, not something you generally do when you are meeting a patient. There is stubble on his chin. Again, not what I would expect from a surgeon starting a clinic. He had a patient scheduled very early this morning. So, it is possible that he has been here since yesterday and didn't have an opportunity to go home. We know he was working late and instructed the staff to leave the lights on downstairs. They were still lit when the nurse arrived this morning. Now, if you think I have done enough of your work for you, may I get back to my own duties?" With a quirk of his eyebrows, he turned away and knelt beside the body.

Downstairs, some of the SOC team were examining the walls, the floors, and the dark-wood desk in the reception area.

A cover was being erected over the doorway to keep out the prying eyes of the crowd already gathering at the end of Rodney Street. The quiet of Liverpool's Georgian Quarter was going to be much more disturbed once word spread.

From the rear of the building came the sound of sobbing and the murmur of voices. Jordan followed the safe route along the corridor and glanced into an empty room halfway along. It was furnished with upholstered chairs and a low coffee table holding a vase of flowers and an array of coloured leaflets. Heavy drapes filtered the noise and light from outside. There was the aroma of freshly brewed coffee.

"That smells good. Shame it'll go to waste," he said to the technician, who was sliding a laptop computer into an evidence bag.

"Yeah, it's not like my doctor's place. You can't even get a drink of water there, or a chair most of the time. How the other half live, eh?"

Jordan nodded. He pointed towards the source of the sound. "Witnesses?" he asked.

"Yeah. Mainly staff members, I think about five of them. All in a bit of a state, from what I saw."

"Has anybody spoken to them yet?"

"Don't think so, very early days. Ted and Vickie have been upstairs and you're the first to arrive from your side."

"Alright, boss," DS Stella May called from the doorway. She was holding up a pair of gloves and some shoe covers, but no suit. "Do I need to clobber up?"

"No, don't bother. We have witnesses to interview. We need to get them out of here as soon as possible."

"I could knock next door if you like. It's another clinic. Their door's open," she said.

"Great, tell them we have people in shock and then give Copy Lane a call. We need more help."

Outside, the early promise of fine weather had given way to drizzle, and Jordan hurried back to the SOC van to take off his PPE and push it into the waiting bin. He paused a moment to take stock and watch as a huddled group was led down the front steps of the clinic and into the building next door, where Stella waited to direct them. Some were in nurses' uniforms, one was wearing a scene suit, and he made a note that she should be one of the first to be spoken to. The only reason she was dressed that way would be because Vickie's team had collected her clothes. He took in a deep breath, glanced around at the fine old buildings, and turned to stride across the road.

Chapter 2

In the clinic next door, the staff room was brightly decorated in neutral colours and furnished with a couple of settees, an assortment of easy chairs, a dining area and small kitchenette.

A group sitting on the small couches looked up as Stella entered the room. A couple were obviously nurses, wearing traditional uniforms of blue dresses and white aprons, one in a darker colour. It was a long time since Stella had seen hospital staff dressed this way and it certainly made it easier to guess who was who. One appeared to be ancillary staff, probably a receptionist, wearing a green dress and jacket with a name badge on the lapel. There was one other young woman in white and wearing a hairnet – catering staff for sure.

A tall woman in a smart, grey business suit stood with her back to the room, staring out at a small back courtyard decorated with large potted plants. She turned, gave a sniff and wiped at her nose with a disintegrating paper tissue. Stella introduced herself and held out her warrant card. The woman crossed the room, took hold of the small leather wallet, and peered down at it.

"I'm the manager of the clinic next door," she said. "Are you in charge? I thought the man, Bliss, was. What did he call himself, the crime scene something?"

"Sergeant Bliss is in control of the crime scene and the immediate actions at the moment," said Stella. "My boss, DI Carr, is the senior investigating officer and will be in charge going forward."

"So, who is going to do what? Actually, what I mean is, who is going to get our place cleared for us to see patients?

Your people are making a terrible mess and wouldn't let us go to our offices."

"Mrs Campbell." The nurse in the darker uniform stepped forward. "I don't think we'll be able to open for a while. You didn't see. It was awful upstairs."

The older woman frowned and shook her head. "But we have patients."

"I know. We're going to have to cancel." The nurse turned to Stella. "I'm right, aren't I?"

"I'm afraid so. It's going to be a while before the clinic can be opened to the public, and certainly not today."

Mrs Campbell began to pace, muttering under her breath. She turned back to Stella. "I don't know what I'm supposed to do. I need someone to help me," she said.

The nurse put an arm around her shoulder. "You need to just relax, Vivienne. You're winding yourself up. You've got this." She paused and took a deep breath and closed her eyes. After a moment, she gathered herself. "Let's just sit down and have a cup of this tea. Then we'll have June start ringing around and changing the appointments. We'll speak to head office and see if we can send our clients to Manchester."

"Yes, you're right. It's going to be so hard, without him, Mr Vance. Big decisions were always made together."

Stella had been taking notes during the exchange and, as the manager sank onto the couch and hid her face in her hands, she spoke quietly to the nurse. "What do you mean, head office? I thought this was a clinic."

"It's part of a chain. There are branches in all the big cities. Birmingham, Manchester, London of course, Edinburgh. The head office is in London. There are a couple of other facilities in this area, one is a hospice, one is more of an inpatient place."

"So, the manager?"

"Mrs Campbell does the day-to-day running of the clinic. Mr Vance has a hand in that but he's also in charge of the medical side. Oh, I should say *was*." Her eyes flooded with tears. She brushed them aside. "Then there's Matron for the nursing and ancillary staff. She's on holiday this week, back on Saturday morning. I'm a senior nurse, Charlotte Burley – Charlie." She summoned up a smile.

"And who's June?" Stella said.

"Senior receptionist." As she spoke, Nurse Burley indicated the woman in the green dress who was encouraging the sobbing woman on the sofa to drink some water. "That other lady is Mr Vance's patient. She's the reason we were in early today. She screamed, and I ran up to the consulting room. I should have escorted her, but she's been before several times, and she knows Mr Vance. When I reached the bottom of the stairs, she was on the landing, hanging on to the banister. I went up just a little way until I could see what had happened." She shuddered. "Then I helped her down, and we rang you."

"Are you going to be okay?" Stella said.

"Yes, of course. I mean, I saw plenty of blood when I was training, but this morning was really horrible. And when it's somebody you know, it's different, isn't it? But, yes, I'm fine and I just want to help."

"We'd appreciate a staff list and contact details for the head office. Could you arrange that?"

"Better if I get June to do it, but I'll tell her. What will happen now?"

"Just leave it to us. You won't be able to go into the building, I'm afraid. We'll need to interview everyone who was in there to start with. We'll need to take fingerprints. That's just routine and for eliminations purposes. I should be able to arrange to do that here, but after that, the best thing would be for you all to go home. Unless anyone needs medical attention. We will be in touch later for certain. If you're up to it, we can take the statements now. It'll save you having to go to the police station."

Vivienne Campbell had joined them and laid a hand on the nurse's shoulder. "Thanks, Charlie. Sorry. I was overwhelmed for a minute. You're right. I'll get on to head office." She turned to Stella. "We need to start letting patients know quickly. Can we do that?"

"Don't tell anyone what has happened at this point. I'm sure you can just say something like, 'unforeseen circumstances'. Appointments get cancelled all the time, don't they?"

Vivienne Campbell drew herself up to her full height. "No. Not here. It's not like that. This is not the NHS. We don't do that." The atmosphere that had been one of mutual consideration soured somewhat, and Nurse Burley withdrew a few steps and gazed down at her feet.

"Oh well, whatever," Stella said. "You do what you need to, but there's nobody coming in, probably for the next week."

"We can arrange for people to be seen at the inpatient facility, can't we?" Nurse Burley said.

"Yes, that's what we'll have to do. You can't have any objection to that, Detective Sergeant?" Vivienne said.

"Where is it?"

"Aughton. It's where those patients who require inpatient care are looked after and where our surgical facility is. It's used by three of the clinics in the group."

"We'll need to speak to the staff there and we may need to send a team of technicians," Stella said.

"Oh, for heaven's sake. You can't do that." As she spoke, Vivienne's eyes filled with tears and she threw her hands in the air.

They all turned as the door opened and Jordan joined them. He frowned at Stella as he sensed the atmosphere and then smiled at the woman standing in front of his sergeant. "I need to know who Mr Vance's next of kin is."

As he spoke, Vivienne Campbell gasped and clutched at her throat. "Oh Lord. Phoebe."

"Is that Mrs Vance?" Stella said.

"Yes. Oh, the poor thing. She'll be devastated."

"I need her address urgently. We don't want her hearing about this through the media."

"We haven't told anyone," Vivienne Campbell snapped.

"Oh, believe me, you won't need to. They're like bloodhounds. There'll be reporters there already," Stella said. "Another reason to get you guys out of here."

"Here." Mrs Campbell held out her phone so that Stella could input the address to her own device.

Once the details had been recorded, Jordan smiled again at the manager. "I need to go back now and speak to people next door. When my DCs arrive, they'll take your contact details and record your statements."

* * *

"Quite an atmosphere in there," Stella said, once they were back out in the street.

"Yes, but you have to sympathise. They've had a terrible shock."

"There's no need to be snotty, though. You didn't hear all that 'we are not the NHS' from that manager woman. Granda had his hip replacement at a private clinic, and they were dead nice and friendly. I bet they only do facelifts and bum plumping here. It's probably not a proper clinic at all."

"Well, you were paying the other clinic, where your grandad was, weren't you? You were a client. Different here; here you're a problem."

"Maybe so, but if any of my lot need stuff doing, I won't be coming here. She's really pissed me off. Snotty cow."

"Let it go, Stel. We need to speak to the victim's wife so…"

"Yeah. It's alright, boss, it's just that I can't be doing with snobbery," Stella said.

Chapter 3

One benefit of having the road closed was that the police vehicles had no problem parking. DC John Grice pulled up to the kerb in his clunky old Ford Focus and he and DC Kath Webster strode over to where the others were waiting for them.

Jordan gave instructions for the interviews and then, with Stella in tow, he set off for Canning Street. It was a short distance and would have been a pleasant walk under other circumstances, but given the rain and their task, they used Stella's electric VW. The address they had been given was one of an imposing terrace of red-brick houses with stone porticos. A pair of bay trees in blue pots flanked the entrance they were looking for.

"You could have bought one of these places with your lottery money," Jordan said, as he cast an admiring glance up and down the street.

"Nah, wouldn't have suited me and there would have been too much house, for just me. I'm happy in my flat with Keith upstairs and the Indian takeaway handy. I wouldn't fit in here. Not me, I'm chavvy deep down," Stella said.

She reached out to ring the bell.

They were surprised by the small woman who answered. She was probably in her mid-twenties. Her hair was covered with a scarf and her blue tracksuit was protected by a yellow apron. She wore pink rubber gloves.

"Mrs Vance?" Stella said.

"Don't be daft. I'm Gilly. Gilly Gudgeon, if you want to be formal. I'm obviously the cleaner, innit." She held out her hands, palms upwards. "Duh. She won't want to buy anything. I can tell you that for certain. If you're Witnesses, you're on a hiding to nothing so…"

Jordan showed her his ID.

"Oh shit. Hang on." Gilly turned and yelled down the hallway. "Mrs Vance, you've got the bizzies. You not paid your parking tickets again?" She turned back. "Daft cow, she's always doing it." As she looked at the two detectives, the smile died on her lips. "Oh God. Something's happened. Has there been an accident?"

Before they could answer, Mrs Vance appeared in the doorway. She was much more what they had been expecting. Tall, middle-aged, but well maintained. Her hair was cut in a bob which swept in a silver curtain to the level of her chin. She was slim and dressed in loose black slacks and a long cream blouse.

"Gilly," she said, "do you have to yell?"

"Soz," Gilly said. "Anyway, the bizzies, like I said."

The older woman turned to the detectives. "Oh, can I help you?"

"May we come in, Mrs Vance?" Jordan said.

"Well, of course. Of course."

As the woman stepped back, Gilly Gudgeon's eyes narrowed, and she pulled off the gloves. "I reckon I'll be off. I've done the kitchen. Back on Monday, Mrs Vance?"

"What? Oh yes, fine."

"Do you want to pay me now? Only I'm going down the shops and I'm a bit strapped."

Phoebe Vance frowned and stared at the cleaner for a moment. "Oh right. Your money is in the jar in the kitchen. Just take it." She turned back to Jordan. "I'm sorry. Look, just come in, won't you?"

She stepped back and led them along the hallway and into a large sitting room. A small fire burned in the hearth and a magazine lay open on the settee.

"You might want to sit down," Stella said.

They did their best to keep the nastier facts to a minimum, simply saying that Roland Vance had been attacked, and that unfortunately he had not survived. The woman glanced down at her hands, which were clasped on her lap. She began to fiddle with the rings on her wedding finger. When she looked up again, there were no tears, just an expression of stoic dignity.

"I am sorry, Detective Inspector," she said. "There has obviously been a terrible mistake. I am not saying it's your fault, but someone is mistaken or out to make mischief in the most awful way."

Stella glanced at Jordan and raised her eyebrows. They had both experienced this before and it was never easy to deal with. Denial was a natural reaction to such terrible news and now they had to go into more detail to help the woman understand.

"I'm afraid there's no mistake," Jordan said. "We have just come from your husband's consulting rooms in Rodney Street."

"But you see, it's not possible. Roland isn't there. He went away immediately after seeing a patient first thing this morning. He'll be in the Midlands by now. He is attending a conference just outside Birmingham at a very nice centre. They have a spa and I am going to join him this weekend. So, I don't know what is going on here, but someone has told you a lie. Who told you it was Roland?"

"One of the nurses. Nurse Burley saw your husband. He was at the door of his consulting room. I'm afraid there is no doubt."

"The stupid girl. She's made a mistake. I'm a little surprised that you have been taken in like this. I would have expected more thoroughness. It's not really good enough, Detectives."

Stella leaned forward and made close eye contact. "There is no mistake, Mrs Vance. There are pictures in your husband's office and our crime scene manager has confirmed that the person in those images is indeed the person who was attacked. I know this is hard to accept, but I assure you there is no mistake," she said.

Mrs Vance stood quickly, taking them both by surprise. "No, this is ridiculous, and I can see that I am going to have to go to the clinic and find out just what it is going on. The next time I meet the chief constable I am going to have to bring all this to his attention. My husband is in Birmingham, and you are derelict in your duty."

"When did you last see him?" Jordan asked.

"Yesterday morning, breakfast time."

"So you didn't see him last night, or this morning?"

"No, I was at the theatre yesterday evening and he was working late."

"This morning?"

"No, that's not unusual. He often leaves before I am awake. He works very hard."

"So, you didn't notice him in bed?" Stella said.

"I beg your pardon?"

"Well, did he sleep in his bed last night?"

"I don't see what that has to do with you. But, since you ask, I don't sleep well, and I take medication. Roland is very careful not to disturb me. He often sleeps in the guest room if he's late."

"So, you can't say whether he came home," Stella said.

"That's enough. I am not going to sit here and answer questions about my private life on the strength of some stupid misunderstanding."

"Is that your husband in that picture?" Jordan asked. He pointed to a framed photograph which stood on the mantelpiece.

Phoebe Vance huffed crossly. "Yes, obviously it is. That was last year at a company ball."

"I have seen the victim at the clinic, Mrs Vance, and I can assure you that your husband has been attacked and did not survive. I am truly sorry."

Chapter 4

Stella was making tea in the sleek, clean kitchen. She found sugar and piled two spoonfuls into the cup intended for the newly widowed woman. She picked up a glass jar of oatmeal cookies. It probably wasn't the occasion to serve snacks. Maybe it wouldn't be awful to just have one while the kettle boiled.

Her deliberations were interrupted when Jordan joined her to say he was going to walk back to the clinic. Phoebe Vance had agreed to the attendance of a family liaison officer once he had explained how useful it would be to keep her informed about what was happening.

"There are no living relatives handy," he told Stella. "She's going to ring her sister-in-law in France and ask her to come. Apparently, they were all very close. It might be a day or two, so the poor woman'll be on her own until then. She's in there now, with that picture on her knee, just staring at it, and trying to hold herself together. I've told her you'll hang on here for the moment."

"So, you don't fancy her for it, boss?" Stella said.

"Too early to rule anything out, but it was a very vicious attack, and she seemed genuinely shocked when we told her about her husband. She's just apologised. Said I must have taken her for a stupid, ignorant woman, but that she truly believed he was in Birmingham. Look."

He showed Stella his mobile where he had copied the booking and travel details from the woman's phone. "I'll have them checked out, but they look genuine."

They took the tea back to the living room. Phoebe Vance had replaced the picture frame and was standing in front of the hearth. She raised a finger and stroked it across the glass, squared her shoulders and took a deep breath. She turned as Stella put the tray on the coffee table.

"We will need to see Mr Vance's rooms here," Jordan said. "His office, if he has one. His bedroom, I'm afraid, and your guest room. People will come later. It may be better if you could stay with a neighbour or someone. It would be less upsetting."

Phoebe shook her head. "I can't. I have to be here. There is no-one anyway. No. There is nowhere for me to go. Carol will come. It will take her a day or so and then we can go to our place in Bath. Will that be alright?"

"Let's take it one day at a time. There is probably no reason you shouldn't go away, providing you keep us informed. For now, I'll leave my sergeant with you until the FLO arrives. Mrs Vance, I am truly sorry about your husband, but we will have to ask you to come and officially identify his body. Will you be able to do that? Not right away, but soon."

She closed her eyes. "Will it be alright if I wait for Carol? I need her with me."

"Of course," Jordan said.

Chapter 5

Jordan arrived back at the Rodney Street clinic to see the coroner's van had pulled as close as possible to the plastic tent now shielding the front entrance. He ducked under the tape and walked to where Dr Jasper was about to slide into his car.

"Ah, Carr. Hold yourself available. My secretary will call you." With that, he sped off, blowing his horn to alert the duty constable to move the tape and let him through.

Vickie Frost walked out of the front door, peeling off her gloves. "Hiya, Jordie." She dragged off her hood and unzipped the suit. "I'm moving downstairs, so got to change this lot. Don't want cross-contamination. You weren't thinking of barging in like that, were you?"

"As if," Jordan said. "I don't enjoy being beaten up."

"Ah c'mon, I've never laid a finger on you."

"Yeah, because I've never come into one of your locations without looking like a Teletubby."

"You! Do me a favour. Nothing tubby going on there. Anyway, I'm giving you fair warning, this is going to be a long job. It's not that the place is dirty, not like some of the shitholes we find ourselves in. No, it's clean enough, but there's people in and out all the time. It'll come as no surprise to you, they refused point blank to give us a patient list. Staff list isn't a problem, but they're going to make us jump through hoops for anything else. Then there are suppliers and whatnot. Anyway, we'll do what we can. We might have a couple of good footprints from the blood upstairs, and I've got people out the back. It looks as though there is some blood in the grass near the door, but it must have rubbed off because we haven't found any beyond the back gate. The grass was wet and effectively washed the shoe soles. We're working on it all. Still doing his office and before you ask, no we haven't found his phone."

"Thanks for that. Is Ted still inside?"

"Yeah."

Jordan rang Sergeant Bliss, who couldn't give him any more information. His patience had been stretched thin dealing with the clinic head office.

"I'm turning it over to you, chum," he said. "I've told them it's a murder and so the rules of data protection don't apply and anyway we'll just get a warrant, but there's no moving them. I've sent a message through to the office to start the application. It would have been so much quicker not to have to do that but, no, that would be too easy. Anyway, we're going round to the doctor's house in about an hour. I called Stella, and she's prepared the widow. The SOC team are not best pleased that the woman is still going to be there. Can you not persuade her to go to a neighbour?"

"She insists there's nobody for her to go to. I'm sorry, you'll have to work around her. I've scheduled a team meeting for three this afternoon. It'd be good if you could attend."

Chapter 6

Jordan spoke with the DCI in charge of the murder team at St Anne Street and they were allocated an incident room and a few spare uniformed constables to swell the numbers. His team from Copy Lane had been cleared to move down to the Liverpool headquarters. It might ruffle some feathers among the city centre staff, but it was so much easier when you could work with people you knew. There was no time wasted getting to know who was going to be reliable and who might skive or stir things among the troops. These first hours were so important that anything to ease the way was essential.

DC Kath Webster, DC Violet Purcell, and the other regular members of the team, were in situ and had already sorted computers and desks for themselves. Jordan moved to the front of the room and waited for a couple of minutes for the hubbub to subside.

"Okay, Kath, what do we know about our victim?"

"I've made a start on gathering information, boss. He's got quite an online presence. I've sent a precis round to everyone's tablet, but in brief. He's fifty-five years old and was what they call a general surgeon. For those that don't know, that's gall bladder removal, hernia repairs, breast operations, all that sort of stuff. He was very well thought of. Oh yes, in case anyone is not up with the jargon, a consultant surgeon is called Mr rather than Dr. Apparently, it's a bit of a status thing so best to be careful. Mr Vance trained in London and then worked in the Far East and Africa for a while. Came back to the UK and moved around a little in the NHS. He started a small private practice about twenty years ago alongside his health service work, and then this group took him on about ten years back. That's when he started making the big money. Moved from his house on the Wirral – he'd been at Clatterbridge Hospital – and bought the place in the Georgian Quarter and a flat in Bath just over a year ago. I checked on the government website and it's well expensive. It's in one of those swanky terraces; he seems to like terraces."

"Yeah, my granny did," John said. "She lived in one in Bootle."

"Not quite the same thing, mate," Kath said.

"Nothing dodgy?" Jordan asked.

"Up to now, it all looks pretty sound. Got good reviews from patients at the clinic. Oh, yeah, he's been married for ten years. His wife's five years younger and a divorcee. Not from round here. There are bits in the media about her charity work – fundraising and stuff. Not serving in a soup kitchen or anything, more like sitting on committees and organising balls. Still, I suppose we all do what we can. Vi's researching her side of things."

Sergeant Ted Bliss gave the team a rundown of what he knew. It wasn't much. They hadn't found a weapon.

"We have requested CCTV footage from all the nearby cameras. There was no CCTV in the consulting rooms, which wasn't a surprise, but there is coverage in the waiting room and reception. Just like the patient lists, the company are refusing us access. I guess I understand, but it just makes everything so much harder. We've requested warrants. One positive is that it's not like the city centre here. The roads are quieter at night, so that might help. His computer from the consulting room is with the technical department, but as usual they're snowed under, so don't expect anything soon. Basically, that's the lot. Not much and nothing, but we're on it."

Ted paused for a moment before making a final comment. "There is a lot of blood. Whoever did this must have been covered. Even if it was very late or early this morning, there was always the chance they could have been seen. If they were, they would have scared the shit out of most people. Like something from a zombie film."

Jordan stepped forward. "We need to search the Police National Computer for any calls that came in about people covered in blood in the area. I would have thought we would have heard already, but you never know. Vi, get on to the *Echo* and local radio. Put out an appeal for sightings. Anything at all unusual. Because we're talking about late night or early morning, it's probably worth talking to sex workers, delivery drivers, cleaners, anyone we can think of who keeps late, or very early hours. John and I will go tonight and have a chat with the working girls. I'll speak to some of the beat bobbies to find out where would be best to start. It's not that far from Rodney Street to many places in the centre and someone on the run could have gone in any direction."

He glanced at his colleague and had a thumbs up in return.

"Right, Stella has tasks for you all. House-to-house mainly. I know it can be tedious, but you just don't know when something surprising will come up, so keep your ears and eyes open. Anything at all you think might be important, feed it back. A couple of you need to go to the other site. It's an inpatient clinic, in Aughton. I don't mind who does it. Mr Vance was normally there twice a week, from what we've been told, and his last visit was on Monday. So, how was he then? Anything different about him and, if you can swing it, details of the patients. To be honest, I imagine that's going to need another warrant, but do what you can. Stella and I are going to the post-mortem exam." He held up his phone for the DS to see. "Message from the morgue. Dr Jasper is fitting us in after five. Now, I'm going back to the widow, check on how she is and see what's happening with the SOC team at the house."

As Jordan left the office, a figure stepped alongside him. He stopped and tipped his head on one side as he looked at her. "I know you."

"PC Sharon Taylor, boss. I worked with you in Copy Lane. I don't suppose you remember, but I was dead chuffed."

"Ah, yes. Got it. You were the one with the ASP in the bin." He recalled a previous case where a discarded gun had been found in a skip and this woman's experience with an extended baton had been useful.

She shook her head and laughed. "Aye, that's me. I was made up when that all worked out for you."

"It worked out for all of us, Sharon. It's a team effort all the way. Your contribution was valuable–" he paused "–and funny, to be honest. Are you based here now?"

"Yep, city centre for a bit. That's what I wanted to talk to you about. You mentioned talking to the working girls. I know you said that yourself and DC Grice were going. But…"

She paused and he could tell she was being careful not to step out of line.

"Yes, go on, spit it out."

"Well, I just wondered if it might be better if I went? I'm not trying to step on any toes, but just thought I'd say – honest to God, boss, I'm not being funny, but I know some of them. I've talked to them, helped a couple of them out now and then, and I just think they might be more willing to talk if… if it's me and DS May. Like I say, I'm not trying to muscle in, but two blokes might be a bit intimidating. Well, I just thought female officers might be better."

Jordan stood quietly for a moment and then nodded. "You've got a point, Sharon. Leave it with me."

"I don't want DC Grice brassed off with me."

"No, it's fine. As I say, it's a team effort always your suggestion is valid. Don't worry. Be ready tonight, and I'll give Stella the heads-up and you can liaise with her. What time do you reckon? Ten-ish?"

"Aye, that should be about right. Not many of them around before that, but before the bladdered boozers get out of the pubs, so they might have time to have a bit of a natter."

Chapter 7

At the doctor's house, the FLO was in the sitting room with Phoebe Vance. The noise of activity leaked from the other rooms, but Phoebe didn't react. A tray of tea things sat on the table untouched. The FLO turned to look at Jordan as he walked in, and she blew out her cheeks and grimaced. He flicked his head to the side, and she excused herself and followed him into the hall.

"She's in bits. Not speaking, won't eat anything. Hasn't made any phone calls, nothing. She simply sits in the chair and now and then she'll listen to the team upstairs and sigh. She's given permission for them to take whatever they want and look at anything. It's hard to even connect with her."

"Poor woman's in shock. Do you think she needs a doctor?"

"I've offered. She's not having it."

"Might be an idea to suggest her cleaner does an extra shift to tidy up. They'll be making a bit of a mess upstairs. It's unavoidable, unfortunately. I've got nothing to feed back right now, but the post-mortem is later today. No need to pass that on. We'll tell her when it's over."

* * *

Dr James Jasper looked tired when he met them in the examination room, and Jordan thanked him for staying late to deal with Mr Vance.

"I didn't do it for you, Carr. He's a colleague and the sooner I have this done, the sooner his wife can come in and get that rotten job over with."

The body was naked on the table with just a cloth covering the genitals. Even from their position near the wall, it was possible to see the multiple wounds. Some were small, not much more than nicks, but several were deep and gaping, the edges torn and ragged. The torso and arms were all damaged and there was a huge slash across the belly.

"Exsanguination," Jasper said. "Of course, I'll do a thorough examination, but look at the state of him. He bled to death. We knew from the mess in his rooms that it was the probable cause of death. Several of the wounds are very deep and may well have killed him anyway, but there was no way he could survive such blood loss."

The rest of the post-mortem followed the routine they had become used to. Everything – wounds, bodily fluids, internal organs, moles, and skin lesions – was measured, and the findings recorded. Samples were taken and labelled to be sent away for processing and then the organs returned to the body cavity before Jasper's assistant repaired the Y incision.

The medical examiner stomped from the room. In the changing area he flung his gown, hat, and gloves into the bin.

"That poor bugger," he said. "That is no way to die, and he put up a fight. You saw the defence wounds on his arms and hands. The weapon was one of those disgusting zombie knives. They've been banned for some time now. They can call an amnesty, appeal to the public to hand them in, but they are with us now. This is the result. A doctor in his own clinic ripped to shreds. Go on, Jordan, get out. I need to go home, collect my wife, and find some peace in the countryside."

"You'll send me a report?" Jordan said.

"Of course I'll send you a bloody report, but not now, not today." With that, he stormed away, leaving his assistant to apologise.

"No need," Jordan said. "It was grim."

He bent to collect his coat, and he and Stella walked in silence along the short corridor to the door. Jordan suggested Stella should go home and have something to eat before setting off again to try to talk to the sex workers in the city.

"So, me and that Sharon?" Stella said.

"Yes, she knows some of the women. You don't have a problem, do you?"

"'course not. Trolling round the city in the rain is my idea of fun, anyway."

"It's not raining."

"Ha, have you seen the forecast?" She held up her phone and showed him the little gif of rain falling on an umbrella.

"Sod it. That's going to reduce the number of people you can talk to, but I don't want to leave it. Time's already moving on, and up to now we haven't got much. I will have to give DCI Adam Trent at St Anne Street a report tomorrow and DCI Lewis is sitting in. God knows why."

"I'm not going home anyway," said Stella. "Too much to do. I'm going to carry out more research on the staff. Me and Kath are sharing them out. Nothing yet, but fingers crossed."

"We need to get a patient list urgently. Could be a disgruntled family member or a patient who wasn't happy with the treatment," said Jordan.

"Yeah, I'll get back on to the head office for the group and start proceedings for a warrant."

"Brilliant. Good luck tonight."

Chapter 8

In Crosby, Jordan's house was quiet. His wife wasn't yet home from her job at Citizens Advice and, with their son Harry still at childcare, he relished the idea of a little while to concentrate on the job.

The witness statements had been uploaded to his computer and there was nothing too surprising in there. Nurse Burley had already told them why they were at the clinic early and that she had run partway up the stairs when she heard the patient, Pauline Griffith, screaming.

Mrs Griffith was a patient who had seen Roland Vance a couple of weeks previously. He thought the problem was her gall bladder. Because she was a friend, he was going to refer her to a colleague and wanted to talk to her about it. His consulting rooms were familiar, and she was happy to make her own way to the first floor. She had seen the body as she turned at the top of the staircase. At first, she thought he had fallen or fainted, but then she saw the blood and she screamed.

Jordan read the report a couple of times and then picked up his phone to call John. "This witness that I asked you to interview," he said, "Mrs Griffith."

"Oh aye. Proper shook up, I understand."

"There is nothing here about how she got blood on her clothes. Her coat and dress have been taken away by SOCO so, did she touch him?"

"I don't think so, boss. One of the uniforms took her statement, and she didn't say she had."

"I asked you to do it. It was obvious she was an important witness."

"Yes, I know, and I meant to, but she was dead upset, crying and what have you, and I wanted to get her done and out of there as quick as I could. I was doing the manager."

"Okay. Well, we need to speak to her again. We need to know just how close she got to the body and whether she touched him. There were bloody footprints all over the landing. Were some of them hers? Whoever conducted this interview didn't do a proper job."

"Have I screwed up, boss?" John said.

"She was an important witness. You should have done this one yourself. Anyway, go see her in the morning and have another talk and find out more details about her reaction."

"Sorry, boss, I can't."

"Why? What are you doing?"

"Well, it's not me, it's her."

"You're not making sense. How do you mean, it's her?" Jordan said. He became aware of the small pain in his hand and realised he was clenching his fist tightly, his fingernails digging into his palm. John was usually much more reliable than this.

"Okay, so the reason Mrs Griffith was in so early to see the doctor was because her husband was taking her on holiday later that day."

"Great. So now we have to go careering across the country or speak to her by phone. This is not good, John. Where has she gone?"

There was an ominous silence, and Jordan felt his stomach clench. "John, talk to me."

"Sorry, boss. She was going straight from the clinic to the cruise terminal. She was meeting her husband and friends down there, ready to board a liner. Like I said, I wanted to get her done and out of there. The woman was in a hurry because of everything that had happened. But I didn't know about the cruise until later."

"What? Where is she, John?"

"Well, by now she'll be on her way to the Canaries. Shit, boss, I'm sorry. I feel like a proper numpty."

"Who told her she could travel?"

"The uniform, I guess. I just said that she could go when she'd signed the statement. I didn't know how far she was going. I just meant she could go home. This is my fault. I'll hold my hands up to it."

"That's going to be of little help tomorrow when I have to give a report at St Anne Street. Shit, John. Oh well, it's done. Leave it with me and I'll decide what we can do."

As Jordan put the phone down, Penny arrived. With one look at his face, she backed out from the room and went to pour him a whisky.

Chapter 9

When Stella and PC Sharon Taylor met at the entrance to St Anne Street, the rain had arrived as promised. The PC was out of uniform, in jeans and an oversized hoody. Her hair was pulled back into a ponytail that flicked back and forth as she walked, her long legs striding out across the paving. After a few minutes, she pulled a lightweight rain jacket from her backpack. Stella didn't normally bother about her clothes and at just over one and half metres, she considered herself average height. She took in the knee-high boots and the skinny jeans of the younger woman and felt short and shabby. It was irritating.

The city centre was almost deserted. There were just a few cars, their tyres shushing on the wet tarmac.

"Alright, Sarge?" Sharon said.

"Yes, fine. This rain isn't going to help us, is it?"

"No, but there're always a couple of girls around and if we speak to them, they can pass the word on. Are you okay with doing this? Only you seem a bit quiet," Sharon said.

Stella turned to look at her. "Sorry, Sharon, what do you mean?"

"Well, I know the boss was going to do it himself and now you're landed with it, the rain and whatnot. It was me that suggested it."

Stella shrugged. "It's the job. I have to say, I've been surprised how often I've ended up wet through and filthy. I thought once I was out of uniform things would get better. Ha, no chance. But if we get something to help, it'll be worth it. Don't worry."

"Sorry, I'm not used to this. Being with senior officers, one to one, like."

"Don't be a div. You know what the boss says. It's all teamwork. It's fairly deserted round here, isn't it? According to my granda, the red-light district used to be Lime Street, by the station."

"Yeah, I know. Used to be. When my mam and dad were young, they said people didn't go there at night, unless they were looking for business. It was dead rough. Not now though, since that's all been redeveloped. Actually, Sheil Road is the place these days – well, these nights, I suppose. But that's too far away from the murder scene, up in Kenny."

"I wouldn't want to be in Kensington without backup at night, so I suppose we should be thankful for small mercies. I never did foot patrol in the centre. There's some rough spots up in Kirkby and Skem but it's not the same, I don't think."

They walked the evening pavements in silence for a while. Here and there a light shone from an office block. From somewhere in a residential development, there was the sound of a car alarm and a dog barking. A uniformed officer on foot patrol passed them and raised a hand in salute.

"Alright, Shas," he said.

"A wet one tonight, Taff."

The bobby nodded and looked up at the sky as if to check that she was right. "Couple of girls down by the multistorey, looking pretty brassed off, poor buggers, if that's where you're headed. I moved 'em on, but they'll be back by now. Only place there's a bit of shelter," he said.

A group of university students, shoving each other into the puddles and laughing, were on the other side of the road as PC Taylor turned to cross. She dragged her backpack from her shoulders, pushed a hand into the side pocket and pulled out a bunch of little coloured packages, holding them up for Stella to see.

"No good bringing them fags these days. That's what the older cops used to bring, but now the girls mostly need something stronger. Obvs all we can do about that is suggest they seek addiction help. They're usually grateful for a couple of johnnies, though, so I always bring some. Here, I get them in bulk from Amazon. Freaked me mam out first time she saw them." Laughing, she passed a handful over. "I can see Suze, over there, and Lena. Do you want to stick together or split up?"

"Let's just stick together. Honestly, I don't think we're going to get much, but at least we can say we tried." She looked around. There didn't seem to be any kerb-crawlers, so the girls would probably be bored and willing to talk.

The two women recognised Sharon, and Stella was surprised when they bent to give her a hug. She gave them the condoms, reached into her bag again for two bottles of water and a couple of bars of chocolate to add to the offerings.

"Who's your mate?" one of them asked, leaning to get a better look at Stella.

"She's my boss. DS May – Stella. We need some help, girls. Nothing for you to worry about."

Even as Sharon spoke, there was a subtle change in the atmosphere. The girls both stepped back half a step and lowered their gaze.

"Don't be asking us nothing that'll get us in trouble, Shas. You know what I mean. I didn't think you did that. We can't dob nobody in."

"No, it's nothing like that. Not really. Look, Tuesday night or maybe very early this morning there was a bloke killed. Not here, over in Rodney Street."

"Jesus, queen, we don't go over there," the one called Suze said, and she nudged the other girl who sniggered.

"Bit high class for the likes of us," she said.

"No, I know, but the thing is," Sharon continued, "whoever did it – the killing – we reckon would likely have been covered in blood. Had to be from the state of the place. So, we just wondered if you'd heard anything like that. Somebody looking as though they'd been in an accident, say. Probably in a hurry. Just anything weird, especially anyone coming from over in that direction. Not many people around at that time, so they'd be obvious."

The girls were already shaking their heads.

"God," Suze said, "that'd be horrible. No, I've not seen nothing like that; have you, Lena?"

Lena pulled a face. "No, I haven't. That'd proper freak me out, that would."

"You haven't heard anyone talking about anything weird going on? Not necessarily here, just around the centre," Stella said.

Again, the women shook their heads.

"Can you speak to some of the others for us?" Sharon said.

"Yeah. If you like. There's not many girls out tonight, though," Suze answered.

"No, we saw that. But anybody you see, anyone you talk to in the next couple of days – just ask, yeah? You've got the number to ring me. If you hear anything, let us know; that'd be sound," Sharon said.

A car had approached while they had been talking, and now Lena moved away across the pavement.

Sharon and Stella turned away quickly and headed down the street. "Jeez, she should know better than to do business right in front of us," Sharon said. "I don't want to have to pull 'em in. Not after all the time I've spent getting them to trust me."

"No, but I suppose it's so quiet tonight she didn't want to miss a trick. What a bloody awful way to live. The council was going to look into making a managed area, safer and better controlled. Surprise, surprise, it never went anywhere," Stella said.

By now they were both wet, cold and miserable. "Sod this. Let's go for a bevvy. We'll do a couple more minutes, walk up past the car park, talk to any girls we see and then straight into the nearest boozer. I've had enough," Stella said.

The pub was full of students from the university, noisy, warm and cheerful. Stella brought them both glasses of white wine and they stood in a corner, instinctively, with their backs against the wall, facing the door.

"Cheers, thanks for this." Sharon raised her glass and took a gulp of wine. "So, come on, Sarge, what's he like?"

Stella raised her eyebrows and shook her head. "Not doing that. Let's just say he's the best boss you could have and leave it. Oh yes, and anything you might hear about him and me – it's absolute utter garbage. I'm friends with his wife and I know his little lad, and anyway he's mad about Penny."

There was no response, and in the dim light Stella could see that the other woman had blushed. "Oh, right, so you've already heard the gossip. People are crap sometimes."

The night had been disappointing all round and now the atmosphere was tense and awkward.

"I think I'll head off," Stella said. "I'm going in early in the morning. It'd be a good idea for you to do the same. We need to get somewhere with this case."

As she turned to leave, Sharon leaned towards her. "Sorry, Sarge. I really am. Are we okay?"

"Yeah. But don't listen to gossip. Police stations are worse than the WI for jangling. Keep your own council. I'll see you tomorrow."

Sharon glanced around the pub and, after a moment's hesitation, she walked across the room to join a group of off-duty officers winding down after a day of work. She'd go in early the next day, but for now, a couple more drinks wouldn't do any harm.

Chapter 10

Jordan sent an email calling for a meeting at seven in the morning and everyone was in the incident room. Most people had coffee, and a couple had brought bacon sandwiches from the canteen. DC Kath Webster had updated the whiteboard with the little they had. Out in the field, on and around Rodney Street, uniformed officers working overtime and some special constable volunteers were searching for the weapon. The contents of the skips and bins were of better quality than in other parts of the city, but it was still an unpleasant task.

Jordan stood next to the window and looked out in the direction of the crime scene. He had already been told that there were television vans parked in the area and reporters from the local and national papers. He sighed. It all made their job harder but it just had to be coped with. He turned back to the room and waited for the hubbub to calm.

"As you can see" – he pointed at the board – "there's a lot of space here. I have a gold team meeting this morning, which is going to be quite uncomfortable. However, that's my problem. So come on, everyone. More house-to-house enquiries and wherever possible, speak to people visiting the establishments on Rodney Street – residents, staff, patients, taxi drivers, cleaners, absolutely anyone who has been there in the last week or so. Ask if anyone was aware of suspicious characters hanging around. People who looked out of place, cars taking up parking spaces without permits. Find the wardens who patrol that street. They'll probably know most of the regulars, so any new vehicles might stand out, especially if there was anyone inside. There are appeals out on TV, social media and in the papers so some of you will need to man the phones. Stella will assign tasks."

He took a moment to look around, giving them time to think about what he'd already said, before he continued.

"The medical examiner said the weapon was a zombie knife. That's not something your average private-clinic patient would have about them, so we're looking for punters who didn't fit in. Let's get on it. I know this happened during the night, but that doesn't mean they weren't there in the days beforehand. John, I need to have a word. The rest of you, that's it, thank you."

Jordan led John to the office he had been assigned and took his seat behind the empty desk. "You messed up here, mate. What have you done about it?"

John lowered his gaze and sighed.

"I've arranged to have a Zoom with her, boss. In about an hour. It may be flaky being on a ship, but they assured me it's possible. She should have received my email with the outstanding questions to make things easier. I'm really sorry about this. I know I should have done better."

"Okay. Keep me informed. Before you go though, John. This is not like you. Is everything okay? No problems at home or anything?"

For a moment, the detective seemed as though he wanted to say something, but in the end, he simply shrugged and said that there was nothing and he'd just made a mistake.

* * *

The gold team members were already gathered in DCI Adam Trent's office. There was coffee and pastries and an air of bonhomie which settled as soon as Jordan arrived. The DCIs from St Anne Street and Copy Lane took seats beside the head of traffic for the area, Sergeant Ted Bliss, and at the end of the table, was the chief constable.

Ted Bliss raised his eyebrows as Jordan turned towards him and pursed his lips. Jordan had expected Trent and Lewis, but the chief constable was a surprise.

Everyone deferred to the most senior officer even though, as SIO, Jordan would nominally be chair. The chief constable asked for a rundown of the current situation. For Jordan, his report felt weak and short on substance, but he couldn't waffle. It wasn't in his nature.

In the lull that followed the brief statement, the chief coughed and shuffled his papers before speaking. "Bad business, Carr," he said. "I knew the victim personally. Our families are friends. I want this solved, and the perpetrator punished quickly. I have heard great things about you. It was my idea to bring you in on this. Don't let me down. Keep me updated." With that, he stood and stalked from the room.

There were some winding-up questions mainly about road closures going forward and manpower, which was, as always, too little and with an eye to minimising overtime.

As they left the room, Ted Bliss caught up with Jordan. "Not a surprise there then," he said.

"What's that?"

"Well, the chief constable, it's the funny-handshake brigade, isn't it? The Masons. Got to be. No pressure, Jordan, but you really are under the microscope now."

"Thanks for that, Ted," Jordan said.

"Yep, you're welcome, mate. Anyway, I have a bit more news for you. I didn't mention it in there because I know that at the moment this might be a bit of a dodgy subject, but we've now confirmed there were two sets of footprints on the carpet. One set was almost definitely male or, if not, it was a big woman. Of course, that's always a possibility that we can't discount. The other set was probably female. We're still working at them to try to identify the type of shoe. It could well be that your cruise lady went nearer to the body than we thought."

"Thanks, Ted. I'll let John know. He's speaking to her later. The SOC team took her clothes. Surely, they'd have her shoes as well." He would need to ask. If they hadn't taken them, it compounded what was already an embarrassing problem.

Stella was waiting in the incident room to give him yet more disappointing news regarding the conversations with the prostitutes. No matter how she tried to spin it with assurances that word was going to be passed around, they both knew they would need to be very lucky if anyone was going to come forward and, as time went on, it became more and more unlikely.

After their meeting, Stella went to join the rest of the team on the streets in and around the Georgian Quarter and Jordan went into the incident room. He opened his computer and brought up the images of the crime scene. He would have to go back to the widow and try to get a better sense of the victim. He wanted to understand just who he was.

Chapter 11

The FLO was still with Phoebe Vance. Carol Vance, the doctor's sister, had pulled out all the stops and flown from her home in France. Though the presence of a family member had helped a little to lift the almost catatonic state of the widow, she was still far from the bright woman who had answered the door just the day before. She hadn't washed her hair, which now hung lank and greasy around her pale, drawn face. She was still wearing the same trousers and top, but now had a thick shawl around her shoulders.

Jordan again wondered if they should call a doctor, but the idea was vetoed. He sat with them in the comfortable sitting room and told them they needed to go to the morgue to formally identify the body and suggested later in the day.

The usual question at this time was how long would it be before a funeral could be arranged, but there was none of that. Maybe their experience on the periphery of the medical field had already prepared them for the idea that it would still be a while. Jordan told them he would try to arrange an interim death certificate so that they wouldn't have to wait until after the coroner's inquest. The reaction was a simple nod of acknowledgement from Phoebe and it was left to Carol to thank him and for the liaison officer to arrange a police car for them to go to the city morgue, just a short drive away, in the afternoon.

Jordan had seen people in shock too many times, but this was a level that he had rarely witnessed.

"Is she like this all the time?" he asked the policewoman.

"Pretty much. Still won't eat, but we have persuaded her to have a couple of cups of tea. She didn't go to bed and won't speak to anyone on the phone. She's devastated."

As Jordan picked up his jacket and stepped towards the front door, there was a clatter from the landing, and he glanced up. "SOC team still here?" he said.

"No, they finished earlier. That's the cleaner. They rang her and asked her to do an extra day. I had a quick word when she arrived, but she just wanted to get on."

"I'll just nip up and speak to her," Jordan said.

Gilly Gudgeon glanced up from where she was wiping fingerprint powder from a door frame. "God, you blokes haven't half made a mess. Was there any need for all this? I mean, he wasn't here, was he? Not when he died, like. Anyway, 'course his prints are here, and mine and his missus."

"Yes, I know. It's always messy. Did they get your prints for elimination?"

"Yes, they bloody did, and they'd better destroy them when this is all finished. I've never had that done before. Made me feel like a proper scuz."

"Sorry about that, but we need to know who's been to see the doctor recently."

"Aye, probably, but it's dead nasty making people do that."

Jordan ignored the rant. He had the impression it was the woman's default means of communication. "On that note, are you aware of any strangers that have been hanging around? In the house, out in the street, anything like that."

"What do you think I am? I'm not the sort who's always gegging in. I mind my own business I do."

"So, nobody then?"

"Like I said, not my business."

"You cleaned the bedrooms on Wednesday morning?"

"Yeah, Monday, and Wednesday, unless they have guests in between, and then she leaves me a note."

"Did you notice whether or not the guest room had been slept in?"

"Not 'specially. I don't go round examining the beds."

"So you would change bedding even if it hadn't been used?"

"Yeah. Like I say, Monday and Wednesday. Bloody stupid, but when you don't have to do the work yourself..." She shrugged. "Not my business, is it? Still, it's their house, their leccy and I get paid whatever."

With that, she turned away, stomped into a bathroom, and he heard the click of the door lock. He glanced at his watch. It was almost time for the Zoom call to the cruise ship and, though he knew it might get John's back up, he had decided to sit in. He couldn't afford any more balls to be dropped right now.

Chapter 12

The internet connection with the ship was surprisingly good. Pauline Griffith sat in the captain's office with her husband beside her. He was restless, shifting things around on the desk and shuffling in the swivel chair. The woman's eyes were bright with nervous tears as she clasped and unclasped her hands on the desktop.

John began by apologising for interrupting their holiday and ignored the humph of irritation from Frederick Griffith. He explained about the footprints and Jordan noted how he covered the poor job that had been done at the first interview, giving the impression that this was completely new information.

"So, as I explained in my email, Mrs Griffith, we need to ask just how much contact you had with the body," John said.

"Contact?" she said. "How do you mean?"

It hadn't been a difficult question and hardly needed clarification.

"How close did you get?" asked John. "Did you touch him? Where did you go afterwards?"

"Go? What do you mean, go?" Pauline said.

"Did you walk across the landing towards the fire escape?"

Jordan shifted in his chair and cleared his throat. This was giving too much information to the witness in his opinion, and John glanced at him and frowned.

Turning back to his notes, John exhaled heavily and straightened the papers. "Just tell us exactly what you did, yeah?"

"I already did."

Jordan couldn't stand by any longer. "Mrs Griffith," he said, "since we last spoke, more information has come to light. This is not unusual in an inquiry such as this. Can you please just answer my colleague's simple questions and then we can leave you to enjoy your holiday?"

Frederick Griffith pushed the chair a little away from the desk and leaned to wrap an arm around his wife's shoulders. "I don't like your tone, Detective. My wife is trying to help. She hasn't been well, and this has upset her deeply. It may be common for people such as you to see hacked-up bodies lying in pools of blood, but for those of us who move in different circles, it's not part of our daily lives. I would ask that you treat Pauline with more respect."

Jordan ignored the comment about 'people like him'. It could be racist, it could be classist, or it could simply be a reference to his job. That wasn't important right now. He nodded just once and leaned in to focus his attention on the woman.

"The questions are straightforward. We need to know whether or not you touched Mr Vance's body and then whether or not you walked across the landing. We are trying to form a picture of just what happened and to eliminate you from our enquiries."

"I didn't. Well, I don't think I did. I saw him lying in the doorway and I thought he had fallen or fainted. I went closer. Then I saw all that blood and I – oh, I think I might have gone a bit nearer. I might have stepped in the mess. I can't remember. I can't. I couldn't look at it. Nobody could look at that."

Now the woman reached and took the handkerchief her husband offered and lowered her head to wipe at her eyes and nose with the piece of white linen.

"That's enough. We're leaving now." Frederick Griffith stood up and reached towards the computer, obviously intending to turn it off.

"This interview is not over. Mrs Griffith, you're an important witness to a serious crime," Jordan said. "I don't want to take further action, but I can insist that you are brought back to Liverpool. You may find yourself accused of obstruction. Now, there's no need for this. We are only trying to clarify what happened. It shouldn't be difficult to answer. We don't think you did anything wrong, so you have nothing to worry about," Jordan said.

Pauline Griffith reached out and laid a hand on her husband's arm. "It's alright, Fred. Let's just finish this."

"No; if they want to question us further, let them get a warrant. We don't want to be involved. Isn't it enough that a friend has been killed without all this?" He turned back to Jordan. "Of course my wife has done nothing wrong. How dare you? I think you would be better trying to minimise the knock-on effects of all this. I believe the clinic is closed. You should try to lessen the disruption. It should be opened again as soon as possible. See to that instead of harassing sick women."

"No, let me, Fred." Pauline turned back to the screen and raised her chin. "I saw Mr Vance and walked a little nearer. Maybe I said his name. I felt dizzy and everything went black at the edges, you know, like when you're going to faint. I had to look away. There was just blood, so much everywhere. That was when I screamed. For a moment, I was frozen. I didn't know what to do. I was just calling for help. Then the nurse ran up the stairs. I managed to get to her, and she helped me back down to the hallway. That's it. I didn't walk about on the landing or go to the fire escape, and I didn't touch Roland. I couldn't, I was too dizzy."

As she finished speaking, her husband reached out. "If you have any further questions, contact my lawyer. I will send his details through." And the screen went dark.

There was a moment of silence before Jordan spoke. "Didn't help that much. Ted Bliss has confirmed that her shoes are in the lab. Even if there is blood on them, it's explained now. We'll wait to see if there's a match to the footprints. But, to be honest, I don't think there will be. On the one hand, it minimises any effect of not doing the interview properly in the first place. On the other hand, it gives us nothing new, does it?"

Frederick Griffith had been angry and confrontational, even allowing for the upset because of his friend's death. Then again, that was some people's default reaction when they weren't in charge. Whatever the cause of his reaction, it niggled in the back of Jordan's mind.

Chapter 13

The team were still out making enquiries and questioning members of the public to find those who were regular visitors to Rodney Street. John went to join them. He had been quiet and had little to say when Jordan tried to talk through the interview with the Griffiths. As he left, Jordan turned on the recording but stopped and watched John walk out of the office, shrugging on his jacket. His head was lowered, and his shoulders hunched. It could just be that he was out of his comfort zone working in the city centre, but that should have given him a buzz. A change of scene from the suburbs was surely exciting. Then again, maybe he felt bad about his mistake, but he would have to get past that. It couldn't be ignored, and Jordan sent a message through on his phone asking the detective to meet him in the pub at the end of shift for a chat.

Jordan had another viewing of the video recording of the interview with the Griffiths. It didn't help, and it didn't settle the feeling that there was something that just didn't sit right. Jordan knew the best thing to do was to let it stew. He went through his notes and then quickly scanned the overnight alerts on the PNC.

At first, there didn't seem to be much to concern him, and he was ready to move on. The name didn't so much jump out at him as slide into his consciousness. A report of a girl's body found in Coronation Park in Ormskirk. Tilly Monk. A girl that he had met when he first came to Merseyside. She was a sex worker and drug addict who hung around the shopping centres in Kirkby. She had been arrested a couple of times and released with a warning, and with some effort they had been successful in finding her a place on a recovery programme. He hadn't heard her name in a while. He was saddened, thinking that it had all been for nothing and she had ended up dead on the street. He had liked the young woman and thought they had helped her. Her body had been brought to the Liverpool City Mortuary. He called to speak to the reception at Pembroke Gardens. There would just be time to make the short walk from St Anne Street.

The female medical examiner Phyllis Grant was slated to perform the post-mortem exam. The thought of that poor lonely woman with no-one who knew her to bear witness to this final insult on her body was too sad. It would take valuable time from his own case, but he could make that up reading any witness statements there might be once he was at home later. Unless the team on the ground found the weapon or there was some other urgent action, he could spare an hour, and he would walk back via the Georgian Quarter afterwards to see how things were going.

He sent a message to John to let him know that something had come up, and he needed to put off the chat until Friday. He received an emoji of a raised thumb in response.

Chapter 14

Jordan hadn't seen Phyllis Grant for a few months. She smiled broadly at him across the examination room and raised a hand. "I thought West Lancs were looking out for this lady," she said. "I didn't know you were covering Ormskirk."

"No, I'm not. You're right, DS Jane Keene has this one. I saw her parking outside."

"Okay, we'll wait for her. How come you're here then? Surely you don't need a refresher course?"

"I met Tilly, your patient, a couple of times way back and I thought we'd helped her out with the addiction and whatnot. I think it's really sad that she ended up like this."

Phyllis frowned and was about to speak when the door opened and the detective from the West Lancashire force joined them.

There was a round of greetings and Jordan again explained his reasons for coming.

DS Jane Keene tipped her head to one side and pursed her lips. "Whatever, sir. I'm more than happy for you to be here. You might come up with some ideas. I'll tell you, this is a bit out of my league. I've seen dead junkies before. We all have, but nothing like this. We know it's become a bit of an epidemic and that, but for fuck's sake, Ormskirk. Yeah, it's busier now with the college and all, but it's hardly a metropolis. It's unsettling."

The body was in the middle of the room on the table, covered with a white sheet. The mortuary assistant pulled the fabric aside. Jordan gasped aloud.

"You alright, Jordan?" Phyllis said.

"Christ. I had no idea. I'll be honest, I didn't read the full report in detail. When I saw the name and where she was, I decided to come along. Stupidly, I made assumptions."

"I'm really sorry. I thought you knew," Phyllis said.

Jordan shook his head and rubbed his fingers over his forehead. The medic took a step towards him.

"I'm fine," he said. "Sorry, I feel like a real idiot. That'll teach me. I just assumed it would be the usual. A sad, dirty body with needle marks and sores. But this…" He swept a hand towards the table.

"Well, I was about to explain when Jane joined us. As far as I have seen, on my first examination at the crime scene, and after a preliminary look here earlier today, this young woman was clean. There are scars which evidence past drug abuse and I'm sure I'll find more of that when I open her up, but no, nothing to indicate that she was using at the time she died. She's a reasonably healthy-looking female – not underweight, decent muscle tone. Her body is clean, and she was dressed in clean clothes. Well, clean of grime at least."

As she spoke, the medical examiner moved to a side table and held up a couple of sealed bags containing a pair of jeans, a cotton jacket, and a bright-pink jumper.

"Her underwear is badly stained, of course, and everything is damaged. But as you see, there are multiple knife wounds. On the torso and limbs and this one across the belly. I don't know if it's any sort of comfort to you, Jordan, but this is not a drug-related death. Poor Tilly was murdered."

Chapter 15

Looking at Tilly's corpse, there wasn't much doubt about what had killed her. As she measured the wounds and examined the organs and identifying marks, Phyllis Grant dictated her findings. A small tattoo of a bluebird on the back of the neck, a healed fracture from a childhood accident, but nothing more of note, except the horrific wounds. She glanced up to where Jordan and Jane Keene were watching. The wounds were deep.

"One of these wounds leads straight to her aorta. She would have bled out very quickly after that. So, we can be thankful that it wasn't too protracted. The poor thing must have been terrified though and there are quite a number of defence wounds on the arms and hands."

"Can you tell what kind of weapon was used?" Jordan asked.

"A long knife with a serrated edge."

"Would you describe it as a zombie knife?"

"You could do, but there are other blades that are similar and I try to stay away from buzzwords where I can. Of course, if we had the weapon, that would be different, but for the moment, I don't want to use emotive terms. I prefer to stick to the facts."

"Fair enough," Jordan said. "There's something here that's making my teeth itch," he said to Jane Keene. "Will you keep me informed, especially if you find the weapon?"

"'course. We've got a team out and we might be lucky. We've asked for CCTV footage. There're a few places with cameras in the town centre, but the park itself isn't covered, not the duck pond and that. The swimming baths have some, but they're in a different area away from where she was found. So, it's all crossed fingers and hoping for the best. It's dark down there at night. I think it's spooky what with the graveyard close by and all, so I wonder what she was doing. I wouldn't be happy on my own. It's the back of the shops and between the main road and Church Street. Nice in the day but at night…" She gave an exaggerated shudder.

"She used to be on the game," Jordan said.

"There's no sign of recent sexual activity," Phyllis said.

"Hmm, it's not a usual hang-out either," Jane said. "The activity at night is in the centre with the bars and everything." She shrugged. "Anyway, this girl. We know she's a Woolly originally – from the Wirral. Her mam and dad are both dead. No brothers or sisters as far as we can find out. We haven't found her phone or her bag if she had one. All there was in her pockets was a return half of a ticket for the train, so perhaps she was living in the city centre, or staying with someone at least. We're waiting for footage from Merseyrail and we will need to go through everything there is from Central Station. It's a lot to look at, but we'll just keep at it. I've had a poster put up at the station and we've had quite a lot of feedback. She was too clean to be homeless, I reckon. Anyway, I'll keep you up to date and I'd appreciate any thoughts. Anything would be useful."

"Of course. You seem to have everything covered, though. I'm impressed," Jordan said.

* * *

When Jordan returned to Rodney Street, there was still evidence of police activity and he spoke to several officers. They were cold and frustrated and probably bored, though they tried to hide that. Everybody wanted to be the one to make a breakthrough, but up to now, there had been nothing. People were still hanging around, intrigued and fascinated by the presence of the press and the police, but apart from a few who used the opportunity to have a rant about the lack of patrols or the parking, nobody said anything of value.

The clinic entrance was still taped off and Jordan spoke from the doorway to a couple of technicians, who were bagging up hairs and bits of dirt from the carpets.

Ted Bliss came to the door, and started to strip off his scene suit. "The place is pretty clean. A team comes in every day, late afternoon, so that's a big help because they'd vacuumed the carpets after it had closed to patients and most of the staff had left. We're not normally that lucky. Anything we do find stands a better chance of being from the intruder."

"Good to know. It's time things went our way," Jordan said.

"Yeah, but it's still going to take a while to go through it all and at the end of the day, it is a high-use building. The cleaners have been interviewed at their offices. They're contractors apparently, and English is not their first language. It's always tricky because they're immediately nervous when police are involved."

"Noted. I'll speak to them. Thanks for the heads-up."

"Yeah, no problem. Now then, I think as far as you're concerned, the footprints are the most interesting. I've made sure you've been sent images. The larger ones are from trainers. Not uncommon, unfortunately. In fact, one of my lads recognised them as the same as his own. They've got some sort of pattern on the bottom. Bloody daft, but it's a help in a situation like this. Well, it would have been except you can get them anywhere in the shops and all over the bloody interweb. Still, it's all information. The other prints are from smoother soles, so could be more formal shoes, boots maybe. They look like they are quite worn from the heel print."

"I'd appreciate pictures of those, soon as," Jordan said.

Ted gave a sharp nod. "On the way. We should be finished here by tomorrow. Vickie has just gone to the chippy for something for her tea, but then we're all off home. The techs are worn out, and that's when things get missed. I'll let you know if anything comes up in the morning. I've got one chap at the house just finishing there in Vance's office. The wife, well, widow, is arranging to go away, and she's been told it's okay as long as you know where she is. That's the lot for now. You know as much as I do, and that's not much. I'm off for a bevvy and a curry."

Back in his car, Jordan called Stella. "I want to question the cleaners at the clinic," he said. "Somebody already talked to them, but I want to have another go. They will have been inside the building while Roland Vance was working on his own. By the way, on the PNC there's a report of a girl found dead in Ormskirk. Have a look at it and I'll ring you later. You'll know why when you read the PM report. I don't want to influence you right now, though."

* * *

As he pulled into his drive in Crosby, Jordan realised he had no recollection of the journey. His mind had been everywhere else. Muscle memory and instinct had taken over. He knew it happened, but it wasn't safe. There was too much crowding his thoughts and none of it leading anywhere definitive. Yet.

Penny was busy in the small office studying for her language exam. Harry had been in bed a while and was fast asleep. He stroked his son's cheek and pulled the duvet tighter around his shoulders. No matter how dark the world became, this little oasis of calm soothed him.

"I've left some dinner in the oven," his wife called. "Won't be long and I'll come through."

"It's okay. I've got work to do. I'm not hungry, to be honest. Will this pie keep for tomorrow?"

"Yep. Just turn the heat off. I'll see to it later."

He had barely sat at the table and pulled his tablet computer from its case before Stella rang.

"Gutted to see that about Tilly. I'd forgotten about her. She was around when I worked in Kirkby. Poor cow. We've got an interview with the cleaners. There were two of them, but they've basically said 'they didn't see nothing, didn't hear nothing'. They didn't go into Vance's consulting room. Apparently, that's the rule. If the doctor is in, they leave it until the next time."

"Okay. We'll speak to them in the morning. Did you notice anything about the post on Tilly, anything that stuck out?"

"Erm, let's see. Stabbed, long knife – I'll bet it was one of those bloody zombie deals, but Phil didn't say so. Oh…"

"Yes?"

"Well, she was clean and hadn't had sex. So, she was either no longer tricking, or she'd hit a dry patch. Is that what you mean?"

"No. I don't want to say too much in case this is just me. Let me sit with it a while. Listen, while I've got you. Have you noticed anything about John lately?"

"Like what?"

"Well, his mood, I suppose. He seems distracted, maybe worried. I asked him if he had anything going on, but he said no."

"To be honest, I haven't been with him much the last couple of days, but I can't say I've noticed anything. Do you want me to have a word?"

"No, it's okay. I'll do it. I'm meeting him for a drink tomorrow."

"He'll have been embarrassed about messing up with that interview."

"Oh, you know about that."

"Well, duh. Everybody knows about that."

"Hm. If he has got something troubling him, that's not going to help. I'll make sure I find time to speak to him.

I'll see you in the morning. Interview with the cleaners and then a status meeting. Can you set that up?"

"Will do."

Chapter 16

The cleaners were both from Eastern Europe. One was a woman in her twenties, clearly upset, and the other was an older man. When they were brought into the police station, Jordan tried to reassure them it was simply to make things easier all round, and they were free to go at any time. The woman, Anna, sniffed and blinked back tears no matter how much they tried to put her at ease and her spoken English was almost impossible to understand. She was so distressed they took them to a family lounge rather than separating them into any of the interview rooms in case the stark surroundings and recording equipment might push her over the edge into full panic. After offering them coffee, Anna began to calm down.

The man, Pavlov – *'call me Paul'* – had been in the country for much longer than his colleague and had a family with him. He relaxed, sipping at his drink and taking several of the biscuits from the tin on the desk. Jordan wondered about the woman's immigration status, but he pushed the thoughts aside. He needed her help, and frightening her even more with enquiries about visas wasn't going to get them anywhere.

Inevitably, it was Anna who had cleaned the first floor where Vance's consulting room was while Pavlov had tackled the reception and examination rooms downstairs. They should have waited for an interpreter, but Anna was in such a nervous state Jordan made the decision to proceed without one. It could come back to bite him, but he had the distinct impression that she was on the verge of running and he had no grounds to hold her. Pavlov agreed to interpret.

Anna insisted she hadn't seen the doctor or anyone else on the night of the murder. She had vacuumed, polished furniture and wiped marks from paintwork. She had cleaned a couple of small toilets, and that was all she could tell them. Yes, she knew Mr Vance was in his room. She kept away and kept quiet. She shrugged her shoulders and sucked at her teeth and then spoke quickly to her colleague. It was frustrating for Jordan to listen to the back and forth and not understand any of it, but now that she was talking, he didn't want to interrupt.

Pavlov nodded and touched Anna's hand. "She says that Mr Vance was unkind. She had opened his door one time before, and he had shouted at her and threatened to call our company. Because she was afraid of him, she didn't clean the floor outside his room, and she didn't clean the banister when he was there. She is worried that now she'll be in trouble."

"Tell her we're not interested at all in how she did her work," Stella said. "We just want to know for sure whether she saw anything that might help us find out what happened to Mr Vance."

The girl drew in a deep breath and grabbed Pavlov's hand. Again, they had to wait until she finished speaking.

Pavlov shook his head and gave a laugh. "Ha, now she is worried that you will think she killed him. Because he had shouted at her."

"Oh, for Pete's sake," Stella said. "Tell her to get a grip."

Pavlov raised his eyebrows. "She understands more than she can speak."

Jordan leaned closer to Anna. "There is no need to be afraid. Nobody here thinks you did anything wrong. Tell me, how did you know that Mr Vance was in his room?"

Pavlov interrupted, "There is a light above the door, a red light to say don't come in." He turned to Anna and spoke rapidly and listened to her response and then shrugged and grunted.

"Huh, I am wrong. The light wasn't lit. The door was slightly open, and she was going to go in, but then she heard him on the phone. She says he was shouting, and she was frightened and so she ran away and finished at the other end of the landing. After a few minutes, she went back to get her cleaning trolley and again there was shouting. Just him, no-one else. He came out of his office and went to the toilet. She hid in a closet until he went back and he slammed the door."

The woman drew in a breath and spoke quietly. "Before the toilet, I hear him say, very loud. Don't come. Not here. Just don't. He use a swear word and then slam down the phone."

There was yet another back and forth of conversation, and Pavlov pursed his lips and sighed. "She had forgotten, until now, she says. After he went to the toilet, he also opened the door."

"Which door?" Jordan asked.

"The fire exit. The one at the end of the landing. It leads to the metal stairs. It is always locked. We have to push the bar to open it. She saw him unfasten the door and then leave it slightly open and then he went to his office. She was worried because that door is supposed to be locked. Sometimes she has taken her cleaning cloths to shake them outside, and she thought she might be blamed. We are told to be very careful about security. It is a clinic. I don't know if there are drugs, but they worry about robbery."

"We'll need her to sign another statement. This time she has to make sure it's all in there – the shouting, the fire door, everything," Stella said. "Come on, I'll take you to speak to my colleague."

Jordan shook hands with both of them. "Thank you, Paul. You saved us a lot of time translating, and please tell Anna not to worry."

Pavlov shrugged. "Ha, she will worry. It's what she does."

Chapter 17

Jordan was happier when he faced the team at the status meeting. They had the information about the fire door and the angry phone call and had already applied for a warrant to access the clinic's phone records.

"I don't expect they'll be happy about it," said Jordan, "but obviously it's essential we have this information, and I reckon it's unlikely to have been a patient he was talking to at that time of the night, especially as he was angry. Kath, can you follow that up? Was it an outgoing call and if not, we need to know where it was from. Kath and Stella have collated the staff interviews from Rodney Street and Aughton and nothing has jumped out as dodgy. They all liked the doctor. He was kind and quiet but sometimes a bit aloof and that was it."

Jordan's phone had vibrated in his pocket during the meeting and when he checked it, there were several missed calls from DS Jane Keene. He went back to his office, and called the West Lancashire station. Jane was upbeat and excited. They had picked up Tilly Mount on the CCTV at Central Station, catching the train to Ormskirk on Wednesday afternoon.

They had followed her progress on the short stroll along Hants Lane and then into the town centre. She had wandered around the shopping area and then headed for Burscough Street and into the Buck I'th' Vine pub. There was no internal video, but it was much later when she emerged. There was no indication that she was drunk, and when she left, she repeatedly glanced behind her and once or twice stepped into a doorway and waited for a little while before continuing on her journey.

"She was on edge. I don't think there's any doubt," Jane said. "She headed back to the town centre from the pub and then walked up Church Street towards the park. We picked her up on a couple of shop cameras but, as expected, once she entered the park, she vanished."

Jordan thanked her. "Keep me in the loop, Jane. I really appreciate it."

Hanging up the call, Jordan waved to Stella from his office doorway and pointed to where John was working at his computer. She nudged the detective constable on her way past and he shut down his machine before he joined them.

"What's happening, boss?" Stella said.

Jordan gave them a quick rundown of the call he had just taken. "They're checking the footage to see if anyone at the train station was seen later in Ormskirk and whether they appear to be following her, but as you all know, that's a long job."

"Sorry, boss. I'm not with you," John said. "Why are we looking at this?"

Jordan took a deep breath. "Cards on the table. It's one of those inexplicable inklings that come along sometimes. I didn't need to go to the post-mortem exam. I just did, and when I saw her body and listened to the findings, it seemed so very similar to the doctor that it niggled away at me. Okay, I know. She's a young woman with a dodgy past and he's a highly educated professional with money and status. There's nothing to link them apart from the similarities between the deaths. Some of the wounds seemed to me to be in the same place. I've sent a message to Phyllis Grant asking her to have a look at the report on Vance. Could be I'm seeing things that aren't there, but I don't think I am. Look, we probably shouldn't invest much time and energy in this right now, but I want to keep abreast of it, and I want you guys to keep it in your minds and if you see anything that you think might be a link, let me know. I know I sound as though I'm rambling, but bear with me."

They both nodded, though John looked very sceptical.

"Oh, about that drink, boss," he said. "I'm sorry, I can't do it tonight."

Jordan waited, but he didn't elaborate. "Well," Jordan said eventually, "I really wanted to have a chat, John. Maybe breakfast tomorrow. I can meet you at that little place in Queen's Square – the charity one."

"Okay. If you like."

It was ungracious and bordering on rude, and the DC's reaction was worrying. Jordan glanced at Stella, who gave a slight nod.

"I can go for a bevvy if you like," she said. "You can tell me more about this woo-woo feeling you've got about Tilly Monk."

Chapter 18

The FLO called late in the afternoon to say that Phoebe Vance was leaving the next morning with her sister-in-law. They were going to the house in Bath and if he wanted to speak to her in person before, then it needed to be today.

Jordan said that he would call in at the end of shift. It was really just a courtesy call to see how the woman was. He didn't have much to tell her. Just repeating that enquiries were ongoing wasn't going to make much impression but there was nothing else, unless Kath could work a miracle in the next couple of hours in her quest for information about the angry phone call. He went to check with her.

"I'm on it, boss. I'm doing my best here but it's blood from a stone stuff. Being a clinic, nobody wants to be the one to make a decision. We've got the warrant, but I'm going from pillar to post. Phone company, clinic, head office. It's like a merry-go-round. In the end they'll have no choice, but why does it have to be so difficult?"

He thanked her and went back to his own desk. He sat quietly for a moment, rubbed his hands across his face and sighed with frustration. There was a subtle change in the light and he looked up to see PC Sharon Taylor hesitating in the doorway.

"Yeah, come in."

She held out her phone and then realised it may not be the most professional move. "Sorry, boss. Only, I've had a message."

"Okay."

"It's from one of the girls in town. One of the ones DS May and me spoke to the other night."

"Yes."

"It might not mean anything. To be honest, it's odd and it might be right off the wall and nothing to do with us. It probably just needs to be passed on really."

"Yes, and…" Jordan grinned at her and she shook her head.

"Sorry, I'm waffling. So, this girl – Suze, her name is – she's down in town, on the game, you know. Well, I asked her to get in touch if she heard anything about somebody covered in blood or anything out of the ordinary or whatever. Well, this isn't really to do with that. But, oh look, I'll just tell you."

"That would be good." Jordan managed to keep the smile on his face, but he was beginning to find her constant prattling frustrating. The more this went on, the less likely it seemed that it might be of interest.

"Well, there's this other girl. She's not been around for a bit. They reckon that she'd got herself sorted somehow."

Right in the back of his mind, a little bell had chimed. Jordan sat up in the chair. "Okay, so…"

"Anyway, they saw her picture on the local news asking for information. Well, they saw her the other night. It was the night Mr Vance had been killed. It wasn't that she was covered in blood or anything like that. She was looking for a friend of hers and was in a bit of a state, according to Suze. They said they just wanted to pass it on and, erm…" She waited.

"Will they speak to me?" Jordan said.

"Yeah, I reckon so. They won't want to come in here, but if we go to them, they might. There's a pub I've met them in now and again."

"Have you registered them as informants?"

"No, God no, nothing like that. It's just that Suze's sister was at school with our kid and I know their mam and I just keep an eye out. I suppose you could say she's a friend as much as anything. That's not a problem, is it?"

"Nope, not as long as you don't cover up any lawbreaking."

"I'm careful about that."

"Right, set up a meeting. Today, if possible."

"So you think there might be something in it?"

"I think there very well might be, and it could be important. Well done."

Chapter 19

There was movement. The conversation with the Griffiths had left him uneasy, and there was this development with the prostitutes. The widow was going away. That seemed odd when she hadn't asked the usual questions about funeral arrangements, but did it mean anything, or was it simply a woman grieving so deeply that she was not functioning properly? They all felt like loose ends.

He texted Penny to let her know that he'd be home late. Stella was already up for a drink, and it would be helpful if she came with him to meet this Suze person. Then there was Tilly. He still hadn't fully shared his thoughts about that with Stella. He was about to leave the office when the internal phone rang.

"Jordie." SOCO Sergeant Vickie Frost was the only person who shortened his name, and it amused him, though it might not be quite so funny if it spread. He didn't feel like a 'Jordie'.

"Hiya, Vickie. You all finished at the clinic? I was there last night. Your people were coming to the end, I think."

"Clinic is finished on site. We've a ton of stuff to get through back here now. A lot has been sent off for testing. But I'm ringing about the house."

"Okay. Phoebe Vance is going away, isn't she?"

"Yes, that's what I've heard. I suppose I can understand it. Anyway, I had my tech stay late to finish. She's a brilliant girl. I have high hopes for her. She thinks things through, you know. Anyway, she has come up trumps, I reckon."

"Tell me?"

"Yeah, I'm going to, sheesh, what are you like? There's another device. A small iPad."

"So? It's not that surprising, is it? Loads of people have more than one."

"Yeah. They do. But they don't all hide them in a false floor in the wardrobe, do they?"

"You're kidding me," Jordan said.

"No. I am not. I have it here in front of me. It's password-protected, of course. I'll admit I had a quick go at logging in, so shoot me. But don't snitch. Anyway, it's on its way down to the technical laboratory now. I'll try and give them a push, but hasn't that DC of yours got a contact there?"

"John, yes, he does. He's dating one of the techs. I'll have him give her a heads-up. This is very interesting."

* * *

John was not at his desk and didn't answer his phone. Jordan sent him a text asking him to contact his girlfriend and see what she could do to rush through the examination of the iPad. There was nothing more he could do with that for now, but it gave him another reason to visit the house in Canning Street.

It was a fine evening and dry for a change, so he walked through the city. It would have been nice to enjoy the buzz at the start of the weekend. As he passed the restaurants and bars, noise and laughter spilling out into the gathering dusk, he realised it had been ages since he had taken Penny out for a meal or even a drink. He had to fix that. She didn't complain, but it was all too easy to be so wrapped up in work and forget to have some time for themselves. When this case was put to bed, he'd ask his sister-in-law, Lizzie, to have Harry for a night and book somewhere nice for a meal. There was a restaurant out near Aughton that had won a Michelin Star – he should push the boat out and treat her for her birthday. It was a couple of weeks away, so there should be time to solve this. Surely, with this latest find, things would start to click into place. Apart from anything else, he had to move things along soon or there would be mutterings from the high-ups.

* * *

The FLO let him in. She was excited about the discovery of the iPad and whispered to him in the hallway. "This is a turn-up for the books, eh? Do you reckon it's important?"

"Let's hope so," said Jordan. "Has Mrs Vance said anything about it?"

"No. It was judged best to let you talk to her first. Is that okay?"

"Absolutely. How is she?"

"Better, I think. She's done some packing for her trip and had a meal with her sister-in-law."

Phoebe Vance did indeed appear to have moved on from the terrible fugue she had been in. Her hair was washed and tied back in a French plait. She had changed her clothes and was drinking tea in the living room when Jordan joined her. She offered him a drink, but he refused.

"I don't have a lot of news for you, I'm afraid," he said. "We are still working as hard as we can and following a number of leads. I have a picture here of a young woman who I think may have some sort of connection with what happened to your husband." He held out a picture of Tilly.

Phoebe Vance took the printout from him and looked at it for a moment before frowning, shaking her head and passing it across to her sister-in-law. "No, sorry. I don't know her. Is she a patient?"

"We don't know that yet. Don't worry about it. The other matter is an iPad that was found in your husband's bedroom."

Again, the woman shook her head. "No, he didn't have computer equipment in the bedroom. Roland was firm about that. He didn't even have his mobile phone in there.

There was an arrangement with the clinic that if an emergency came up, they would use the landline. It was one of his foibles. Something about blue light and sleeplessness. He didn't even like me having my Kindle in there. No, there's been a mistake."

"The iPad was hidden." Jordan made the bald statement and waited.

Phoebe screwed up her nose and glanced at Carol sitting in one of the easy chairs. "Hidden. How do you mean, hidden?"

"It was found under the floor of his wardrobe."

"Ridiculous."

"Have you been in the bedroom?"

"No, they wouldn't let me in there. I've been using one of the guest rooms."

"Shall we go and look?"

With a huff and a twitch of her shoulders, Mrs Vance stood and followed Jordan, waving her hand at the sister-in-law to stay where she was.

The SOC team had left a small tent-shaped marker at the door of the wardrobe. He pointed to the base of the cupboard and the two boards that had been lifted to reveal the space underneath. He wasn't sure what to expect as a reaction, but Phoebe simply raised her eyebrows, sniffed and turned away.

"I know nothing of this," she said. "I can't imagine what it means. I'm sorry, I just can't help you."

She pushed past Jordan, and he heard her descending the stairs. He took a couple of pictures with his phone, though there would already be some in the files, and went back to join the women in the living room.

Seeing that he was on a hiding to nothing, Jordan made sure to take the landline number in Bath and the address and told Phoebe he would inform her of any developments.

Stella was waiting in the street outside, eating a sausage roll. She held out a greasy bag. "I was starving. Thought you would be as well. Not healthy, but it'll soak up any alcohol we might have later and give you a boost."

Jordan peered at the fatty, flaky pastry and slightly grey meat. He cringed to think what his mother and nana would say and then bit into the snack with a small groan of pleasure.

"You already spoke to these women? The streetwalkers," Jordan said.

Stella couldn't speak with her mouth full and simply nodded at him. He didn't want to spoil her enjoyment of the wicked snack and so they turned together to walk towards the pub where the girls and Sharon were hopefully already waiting.

Chapter 20

Sharon jumped up from her seat as Jordan and Stella pushed through the pub doorway.

"I'll get your drinks in, boss. What are you having? Suze and Lena are on the way." She pointed to the table where two glasses of white wine and a pint of beer dribbled condensation onto the stained, dark wood.

"That's them now." She raised her hand to wave to the two young women at the door.

Once the introductions were taken care of and Jordan's lager and Stella's cider had arrived, Jordan held out the picture of Tilly.

"So," he said, "first of all, is this who we are talking about?"

Suze took the image. "Yeah. That's T. She's dead, isn't she? That's what the news said."

"I'm afraid so."

"So, if she's dead, why are you lot interested? Just saying. I mean, there's homeless people and women like us dying all the time, there isn't always this fuss. No offence, like, but why her?" Lena said.

"Because she was killed. She didn't die of an overdose, or illness, nothing like that. Somebody deliberately murdered her," Jordan said.

"Shit, poor bitch." Suze sniffed and wiped at the corner of her eye with a finger end.

"Do you know if she had any connection with Ormskirk?" Jordan asked.

"Ormskirk, no, why would she? She was a Woolly and then after she came here, she had a place in Bootle, worked out in Kirkby; keeping it away from home, you know. She was often in town back in the day. Then she wasn't around anymore. We just thought she'd moved on. She used to talk about going to London, but, Ormskirk, that's out in the sticks," Suze said.

"Okay. So, you don't know where she was living?"

"No, as I say, she hadn't been around for ages. That was why we noticed her the other night."

"I saw her down the shops a couple of times," Lena said.

"You never said." Suze gave her slap on the arm.

"Well, she didn't speak. To be honest, I thought she was trying to swerve meeting up. You know, thinking about it, she did go over to Ormskirk sometimes, back in the day."

"She never," Suze said.

Lena frowned at her friend. "She did, I know she did. She had that old aunty that used to live out there. Aw, come on. You remember, you must do. She went that time when she'd been poorly. Stayed out there and said it was boring as fuck. Wasn't even a proper aunty, just a friend of her mam."

Suze nodded slowly. "Oh, yeah. But she was well old. She must be dead by now."

"Can you remember her name?" Stella asked.

Lena took a sip of her drink before replying. "Not really. She was Aunty Bev, I think. That was all I knew. I think she lived in a pensioner's bungalow. Like I say, she must be dead by now. That's yonks ago."

"That might be a help, though, thanks. You didn't mention that you'd seen her when you spoke to Stella and Sharon," Jordan said.

"No, why would we? They was asking about people with blood on them and stuff. She wasn't covered in no blood. All she was doing was looking for her mate. Okay, she was a bit hyper, but I just put that down to her being back on the gear. Ha, or off the drugs."

"Who was the mate she was looking for?" said Jordan.

Suze and Lena looked at each other and it was Suze who answered. "A girl called Bren. I think it's Brenda, but it might not be. Anyway, she was a mate of Tilly's. Come to think of it, I hadn't seen nothing of her for a bit either; had you, Lena?"

Lena shook her head.

"Did Tilly say why she was looking for her?" Jordan asked.

"No. Hey, any chance of another of these?" Suze held up the empty wine glass and Stella rose immediately to bring another round, less her own and Jordan's.

"So, you were saying you hadn't seen this Bren for a while." Jordan had to keep them talking. Once the drink ran out or they became bored and the streets outside became busy with potential clients, they would be gone.

"No, not for a few weeks. She was doing okay. Got herself clean and sober and cut back on work. I thought she'd found someone to live with, or, you know, one of them sugar daddies." Suze sniggered and nudged her friend.

"She might have, though. She was only a kid really, and she was dead pretty," Lina said.

"But you haven't seen her lately?" Stella said.

The two women shook their heads.

"Like we told Tilly that night," Suze said, "we hadn't seen her. That upset Tilly, that did, and she went off. She asked us to let her know if we saw Bren and that was it. Like I say, she was in a bit of a state – snivelling, actually. But she went off, and that was that. Don't know how she thought we were going to let her know. She wasn't making a lot of sense, to be honest."

"Did you see where she went?" Jordan said.

"No, she just went off scuttling down into town," Lena said.

"Scuttling?" Stella said, raising her eyebrows.

"Yeah, she weren't hanging around. Well, she looking for her mate, wasn't she?"

"Was she worried, or was she more afraid?" Jordan asked.

"Ha, afraid! Do you know what we do?" Suze said. "Everyone's always afraid. We might tamp it down, like. Keep it under control but honest to God, we're always afraid of something. But I'd say she was worried and I reckon she was scared."

"Do you know Bren's surname?" Jordan said.

Suze frowned. "I think it was another B word, Barker maybe, or maybe Baxter. Yeah, probably Baxter."

Chapter 21

Jordan and Stella walked back to St Anne Street in silence. As they entered the car park, Jordan stopped, stuck his hands in his pockets, and leaned against the wall. "Did that help much?" he said.

"I reckon it was worthwhile. We can place her in town on Tuesday night and we know what she was doing, and that it was getting her upset. We can pass on the information to DS Keene about the old aunty, not that we have much to go on. Could be a bit of help for her, I suppose. But, boss, what is it that's driving this? I mean, I guess it's one of your 'feelings' and I respect that because they've been spot on in the past, but this has got me puzzled. Why are we chasing round after this woman?"

"Yeah, sorry. I suppose it seems a bit far out even for one of my 'feelings'." He flicked air quotes as he spoke. "I just keep seeing images in here." He tapped his temple. "Vance and Tilly's wounds were so similar. Okay, a stab wound is a stab wound, I get that, but they were the same size and almost in the same places on the bodies. If I was asked, I would have to say it was the same knife. I know I'm not an expert, but we've all seen plenty of knife wounds, haven't we? I'm waiting for more information from both Phyllis and James Jasper about the height of the assailant and all of that, and I believe they're conferring now. They should have something tomorrow. And yes, I know it's Saturday, but I don't think we can take the weekend right now."

"No, that's okay. Have you spoken to John, by the way?"

Jordan shook his head and pulled out his phone to scroll through the messages. "Nothing. It's off, is this, and I could do with his help getting that iPad fast-tracked."

"Leave that with me. I've got a contact in the lab. It'll cost us a bottle of rum, but you must have a couple spare round your place."

"I have as it happens. Brilliant. Can you contact Kath? I want her looking for this Bren. I reckon that'd move things on."

* * *

Phyllis Grant rang later that evening. She was amused by the reaction there had been from James Jasper at his holiday cottage.

"That man kills me. He started off ranting about never having a moment's peace and all of that, but once we were involved in the discussion, he was absolutely focused bringing up reports on his computer and referring to old records. Then I heard him shouting to his wife that he couldn't possibly do the cocktails because he was busy. He added a 'darling' on to the end of that – wish I'd thought to record it."

She laughed.

"Anyway, we are both on the same page and I have to tell you, Jordan, you have gone up in his estimation, and that's quite a feat."

"Good to know," said Jordan.

Phyliss chuckled again. "Well anyway, we agreed that the murder weapon in both cases could have been the same; if not, it was very similar. Of course, the two conclusions lead in different directions. I get that, but that is our thinking. More importantly, from your point of view, I think is the pattern of wounds."

Jordan could hear the click of the keyboard.

"You were spot on, Jordan, allowing for the difference in build and height of the victims, which was considerable, the pattern was similar enough to lead us both to think

74

that they could more than likely have been delivered by the same person following some sort of – oh, what shall I call it – a routine? We can make a decent estimate on the order in which the wounds were inflicted, and that's what we have used. Imagine a dance, a deadly dance, with a nasty long-bladed weapon and the moves in both cases were the same. Why and how, is not our problem, thank goodness, but I really wish you well trying to make sense of this and if I can be of any help, then please, reach out."

Jordan ended the call. He wasn't sure how he felt that he had spotted this similarity. There was relief and some satisfaction, but it was confusing. At least now, he wouldn't have to explain why he had spent time on a case that was being handled by another force. As he drove home, he called Jane Keene, Stella, and John with the news. The DS from West Lancashire promised to have the photograph taken to the various old people's accommodations, but no-one held out much hope of finding Aunty Bev.

"It's something though, sir," said Jane. "At least we have an idea why she was in the area now."

"Not if the aunty is dead."

"It might simply have been the first place she thought of to get away from Liverpool."

"Possible. Let me know if you have any luck."

"Of course."

He left a message for John but also a demand that the DC come in to see him before the status meeting in the morning. He was both worried and angry. If there was a problem, then there were systems in place to deal with them but, apart from that, it was hurtful. He thought of his team as friends as well as colleagues, and if a friend was keeping secrets or struggling alone, there was something badly wrong.

Chapter 22

Jordan was in the office by half past six. He made coffee and brought bacon baps from home, but by half past seven when the rest of the team began to arrive, John had still not shown his face.

While he was waiting, Jordan had printed a couple of the images that Phyllis sent through late in the night. She had done a wonderful job of comparing and marking the wounds on both victims, and noting the order in which they had been inflicted. Seeing them in hard copy in front of him, the pattern was even more obvious. He wrote a brief report on the findings for the attention of DCI Josh Lewis and the other members of the gold team. It would hopefully hold off any irritation with lack of progress.

There was a buzz in the room as everyone saw the images and realised that they had a crossover between the two cases. Nobody was surprised when they were told Jane Keene would be joining them.

John crept in at the back just as Jordan began explaining how the co-operation between the two forces was going to work. He would be SIO, but it was stressed that this was no reflection on the work done by DS Keene. Of course, everyone knew she would be smarting a bit, but she covered it with good humour, and she'd brought doughnuts.

"We haven't had any luck tracing Aunty Bev," said Jane, "but I've got a piece in the local paper and posters up everywhere. Mind you, we have CCTV footage of Tilly from the moment she left the train station, and apart from the pub which we've already canvassed, she didn't go anywhere except the streets and the park."

Stella began assigning tasks and Jordan stomped up to where John was turning on his computer and stowing his backpack.

"My office, now, please."

John pushed the door closed behind him as he entered. Before Jordan had time to speak, the DC held up his hands in a gesture of submission.

"Boss, I'm sorry. I know I've been out of line, but hear me out, please." As he spoke, John lowered himself onto the visitor's chair and blew out his cheeks.

"I've been waiting to hear you out for two days now, John. You know this isn't on. Okay, so why have you been out of touch? I sent texts, I left messages, I phoned."

"Can I just say that it's personal?" As he muttered the question, it seemed that he already knew what the response would be and the DC shook his head before he looked directly at Jordan.

"How do you mean, personal?"

"It's something I don't want to talk about right now. I can't."

"If it's interfering with your work, your reliability, then, no, you can't just say it's personal. I thought we were mates. Is it so bad that you can't tell me? You know I won't tell anyone if you don't want me to, surely."

"Can you just give me some space? I won't let it interfere anymore. I'll be here and I'll do my job, but just give me some time, yeah?"

"Is it something that could land you in trouble?"

"Ha. No, not trouble with the job, anyway." John stared down at his shoes.

"Well, I don't see I have much option. I want you here though, John; completely here, mentally and physically. If you can't do that, then tell me now and we'll have to make some decisions about what happens next."

"I will, boss. I'm on it."

"Okay, the technical lab sent something through. Stella had a contact who worked late, and he's sent a file that he thinks we should look at. Have a gander at it and give me a rundown on what it says. It's some sort of spreadsheet, and I didn't have time to study it. I'm going back to the Vances' house. The cleaner is going to be there, according to the FLO, and I want a word with her while Mrs Vance isn't around. John…" Jordan waited until the detective constable was looking at him again. "I'm here if you need to talk to anyone."

"I know, boss. Maybe later, like, when I've got it sorted."

Chapter 23

Stella was trying not to be too obvious, but Jordan knew she'd been waiting for John to leave the office. He smiled to himself when it took her a brief three minutes before she appeared at his door.

"All okay, boss?" she asked.

Jordan sighed. "Not really, no. He's got something going on, but he won't say what."

"What's the plan?"

"No plan, to be honest. I've left it with him. Anyway, I've tasked him with reviewing that file from the technical lab. It needs a proper study, and I haven't had time yet. I hope he'll be able to come up with an idea of what it all means. It's got to be important and surely there's something about it that's dodgy. You don't hide a tablet computer under the floor of the wardrobe if all you've been doing is scanning your Facebook posts."

"Maybe something like a bank account he didn't want the wife to know about."

"Yep, I had already considered that. It doesn't look like a financial account, though. Not unless it's some sort of code, in which case we'll have to get help from the university, maybe their maths department or the force forensic accountants, that sort of thing. For now, I'm going to have a word with their cleaner. Maybe with Mrs Vance away, she'll be more forthcoming about her employers. They see everything, don't they, cleaning staff?"

"Do you want me to come with?"

"If you've got time, I'd appreciate that."

"I'll pass on what I was doing to Vi. I was still collating witness statements and cross-referencing the ones from Rodney Street with those from the clinic in Aughton. Well, I should say I was doing it again. It's boring and the ones from the inpatient place didn't give us anything of interest, but Vi seems to enjoy it. I'll be more than happy to swerve it." She held up her hands, palms outwards. "I know, I know, it's all necessary and answers are often hidden in details, but it's still bloody boring."

Jordan laughed. "Yeah, okay. We'll take your car. Well, we will if the thing's charged up."

"Aw come on, boss. It's only been a couple of times it's been low on leccy."

"Yes, but my old-fashioned petrol vehicle is always available."

"Well, okay then. We'll take yours."

"Ha, touché. Tell you what, it's not far. Let's walk."

* * *

Gilly Gudgeon answered the door quickly with her earbuds in, swaying to her sounds. It was obvious they didn't have all her attention.

She didn't wait for them to speak. "She's not here. Thought you'd know. She's gone off with that woman from France. Bath, or rather Baaarth." She giggled and pulled the phone out of her pocket to silence the music. "Before yous ask, no, I haven't a scooby when she'll be back."

"It was you we wanted to talk to," Stella said. "Can we come in?"

"No. I'm busy. You'll have to make an appointment. I've got the whole place to turn out. All his clothes to bag up for the Sally Army shop and I'm not allowed to sort out any for myself. As if my fella would want his poncy stuff. I suppose she thinks I'll sell 'em. I would've as well. How's she gonna know, eh? Her with all her charities, coffee mornings for this one, wine and cheese tasting for that. We had the mayor here a bit since. All sorts of stuff, name in the paper and pictures in the *Lancashire Life* at balls and what have you. And I can't even take his old jacket for my fella to do the garden. Anyway, she's left a list so I'll have to get on."

"We'd still like to come in for a word. I really don't want to ask you to come to St Anne Street and I know you don't want that, so…" Jordan shrugged.

With a huge sigh, the young woman stepped back, swung open the front door and, with a mock bow, ushered them into the hallway.

"Shall we sit in here?" Jordan said, stepping towards the living room.

"You're kidding. I'll go up in smoke if I sit on them chairs. She'd know no matter how far away she is. Bloody witch. No, let's go in the kitchen; I'm allowed to sit in the utility room for me cuppa. Do yous want one? I'm not making you that swanky tea with plant bits floating in it, but you can have a cup of instant coffee if you like. That's what I'm having."

Stella agreed to the coffee. Jordan asked for a glass of tap water. Neither of them wanted, or needed, a drink, but it was a way to put the meeting on a more friendly footing. If they could get past the prickly attitude, then there was more chance that Gilly would chat.

"How long did you say you've worked here?" Stella asked.

Gilly scratched at her neck and puffed out her cheeks. "Tell you what, let's not mess about. Yous say what you want to know, and I'll tell you if I can help. I can't be arsed with pussyfooting around."

The statement left them both off balance for a moment and it was Jordan who broke the silence. "Okay, fair enough. First of all, what was the Vances' marriage like?"

"How d'ya mean, what was it like? It was like any marriage. They were alright sometimes and other times they was like wild dogs yelling and screaming at each other. Just like any couple."

The idea of screaming at Penny like a wild dog was so incomprehensible that Jordan was lost for words. What was worse was that this woman believed that to be a normal relationship.

"They had rows then?" Stella said.

"Exactly. Then one or another of 'em would stomp out of the house or upstairs and there'd be an atmosphere for days. It was horrible sometimes. But that's what people are like, aren't they? What can you do? I just keep me head down and take the money. The money's good, and they pay me on time. Never any problem with that, so the rest of it was none of my business. If she moves away permanent, I'll have to find something else and I don't want the hassle so I'm hoping she stays here."

For a short time, there was nothing but the sound of the birds in the garden and the noises of the old house adjusting to the changes in temperature. The officers gave the woman time. Gilly slurped at her drink.

Stella leaned forward to put her empty mug on the table. "These arguments, how often did they happen?"

"Well, I don't know, do I? I'm not here every day." Gilly paused and carried the two empty mugs to the sink, where she rinsed them and placed them on the draining board to dry. "It was getting worse. I will say that. It got so that nearly every time I come in, one of them'd be in a huff or she'd be slamming round the place in a strop. 'course he was at work a lot. But yeah, it was getting worse, and she was going off down south more than she used to. It's alright if you're not working, isn't it? Some of us would love to go swanning off, but we have jobs to do and kids to look after. Anyway, I reckon it suited him."

"What did?" Jordan asked. "What do you mean?"

"Well, let's just say that when the cat was away, the mouse was dead chuffed."

"Do you mean he was having an affair?" Stella said.

"Dunno, do I? Don't know what you'd call it. All I know is that when I come into a house with one person living in it, there were a lot of glasses and if he were polishing off that many bottles of wine, he shouldn't have been cutting people open the next day. I was surprised they stayed married, but you can't tell with rich bitches, can you? They'll put up with anything to keep on getting the jewellery and handbags. Then again, maybe she loved him and it was just their way."

"What about his computer?" Stella asked. "He had at least one, didn't he?"

"'course he did. Who doesn't? I think he took it to work with him. It was only in his office if he was home. She had a laptop that she put on the dining table. Hey, but I never looked at them, if that's what you're insinuating. I didn't never do nothing like that."

"Did you ever see one in the bedroom?" Jordan said.

"Nah, they had books in there, that was all. She had novels, Jilly Cooper was one, I've read hers myself. But he had like textbooks for medicine and that. Never no computers that I saw."

She stood and opened a large cupboard in the corner.

"I'm not saying no more. It'll only come back to bite me on the bum, and I need this job. I think I'll keep me gob shut." She made a zipping motion across her lips with a finger and thumb. "Other people's marriages are their affair and hard to understand and that's that."

She had suddenly decided that she wasn't a gossip and so when she dragged the vacuum cleaner out of the cupboard and began unwinding the flex, they decided there was no point staying. What they had heard wasn't evidence of wrongdoing, it was little more than hearsay and assumptions.

"If you're holding something back that might help us, you could be in trouble," Stella said.

"Like I say, I don't go poking my neb in, so that's me finished."

"We might need to speak to you again. Would it be best if we come to your home?" Jordan asked.

"Christ, no. You do that and my old fella'll be miffed for weeks. We don't want no bizzies round our place. No way."

"Okay, here then. What days will you be coming?"

"I don't know, do I? She just says to do two days a week to suit meself until she lets me know she's coming back. Can't come back to no dust, can she? I'll give you my number and you can call me. I hope you don't though. I'm done talking about them."

* * *

Back out on Canning Street, the cloud had cleared and there was a gentle breeze from the river. "Fancy going back the long way?" Jordan said.

They walked down Upper Duke Street with the Anglican Cathedral, towering on the left, the red sandstone glowing in the late summer sun. To avoid the town centre and the Saturday crowds, they followed Duke Street onward to Canning Place. When they reached the waterfront, Jordan bought them takeaway coffee from a café in the Albert Dock and they leaned on the railings in front of the apartments. It was busy but pleasant to be near the Mersey with the hum of the city behind them.

"You know, for me, it just doesn't gel," Stella said. "The way she was – Mrs Vance – gutted and that. If Gilly is right and they were at each other's throats all the time."

"Oh, I don't know," said Jordan. "Some people thrive on conflict, though. Maybe that was just what worked for them."

"I'm not buying it. If the cleaner was right and she was just putting up with it for what she could get out of him, why did she react like that when he was killed?"

"What's more interesting, I think, is the idea that he was entertaining people while she was away. Who was that? Did his wife know? It could have been quite innocent but if there are extramarital affairs, we could be looking at jilted lovers, jealous rivals and that sort of thing. I would like to speak to Carol Vance on her own as well. I don't want to bring her into the station so as soon as they get back from Bath, we'll arrange to see her. We need to speak to people who knew Mr Vance. Maybe the clinic staff, the manager, the senior nurse, or even the patient who found him. The Griffiths knew him socially. Could be what Ted Bliss suggested; the husband looked the type to be in the Masons."

"How d'ya mean?"

"I don't like that old school tie and who you know sort of thing, but it exists. If he was hiding things from his wife, would his friends know and cover for him? It's a different world for wealthy, entitled people. I think they have different standards. Probably they're not all like that, but it's what it always seems like to me. Their relationships seem different a lot of the time. You know, not the same as the rest of us, ordinary working people."

"Oh yeah, that's just reminded me, talking about working people, there's no interview with the matron."

"No. She was away, wasn't she? I think she should be back by now," Jordan said.

"Yeah, I think so. She might be one of those who knew him well. It would be good to have a word anyway, just for background."

"Good thinking." Jordan glanced at his watch. "Let's see if we can arrange that this afternoon. Then why don't you come back with me to Crosby? We'll have something to eat and chill for a while, see if anything shakes loose away from the office. Penny'd love to see you."

Chapter 24

The matron lived a short distance out of the city centre in a bay-fronted, three-story house opposite the Botanic Gardens in Wavertree. The woman who answered the door was tall and slender. Jordan judged her to be in her early fifties or maybe a little older, but clearly looked after herself. Her dark blond hair showed no sign of grey, but it was difficult to say whether it was the skill of a hairdresser or just good genes. There were faint lines around her mouth and others more pronounced at the corners of her eyes. She looked tired and irritated.

"Ms Rose Heath?" Jordan said as he held out his warrant card for her to inspect.

She glanced at it briefly. "I've been expecting you to contact me ever since Charlotte rang me with the news."

"We waited until we knew you were back from your holiday," Jordan said. "Where is it that you've been? Nobody seemed very clear."

"Well, I only arrived a couple of hours ago. I've been in Europe. Can't this wait? After all, nothing I say is going to change anything. I'm very tired and I need to sort myself out." She swept a hand down the front of her travel-stained clothing. Her cream linen blouse was creased, and the heavy cotton trousers had a mark where something had been spilt. "I need to get a wash on and have a nap. I'm going to the clinic later. Oh, I suppose that's alright, isn't it?"

"Yes, we've finished there, but it's the weekend. You're not open, are you?" Stella said.

"No, there'll be no patients. But there must be a lot for me to do. I can't begin to imagine what sort of condition

86

the place is in. Charlotte said there was blood everywhere and then you people made even more mess."

"Unavoidable, I'm afraid," Jordan said. "We can arrange for specialist cleaners to come in."

"Good grief, no. Your so-called specialists have been in already and now I need to make sure the job is done properly, to our own somewhat higher standards. Then I have to go to our inpatient clinic. There is a management team, but after what happened, I need to show my face. I believe you even had people out there disrupting things."

"We tried to keep disruption to a minimum and I understand there are no inpatients now."

"No, none of ours, of course not. You made it impossible for us to function."

"I would say that whoever killed Mr Vance is the one who has created these problems," Jordan said.

There was a tense silence and then the woman's shoulders slumped, and she turned and led them into the living room. "Let's get it done then," she said.

The room was chilly, but the gas fire had been lit and as Jordan walked past the radiator, he could feel heat. An empty cup and a plate sat on the coffee table, and an open suitcase lay on the floor surrounded by heaps of clothes and several small, zippered holdalls. A pile of coloured folders were on the table.

She didn't offer them seats and remained standing herself.

On the mantelpiece were a few framed images. Mostly they were groups of women in older-style nursing uniforms, but one was a mixed group.

Jordan stepped closer. "Is this the clinic?" he asked.

"Yes, not long after we opened."

"So, you've been there from the beginning."

"I have. Mr Vance gave my name to the company and when they saw my CV, they were more than happy to recruit me. I had been a senior sister in a private hospital for a few years. I trained at the Royal in Liverpool."

"You're not from here, though, are you?" Stella said. "Least if you are, you've lost your accent."

"I went to school in Wales. Boarding. My parents were abroad. Daddy was a doctor in Africa, Asia, the Middle East. Mummy was a secretary, but she could always find work wherever he went. A British education can take you a long way."

"Okay. So, where was it you said you'd been?" Jordan asked.

"Europe."

"France, Germany?"

"I travelled extensively."

It was like trying to get blood from a stone, and Jordan wasn't prepared to waste time sparring with this woman. "Had you known Mr Vance for a long time?"

"I had. I first met him when I was training. We came across each other now and then. I was a surgical nurse."

"Do you know his wife?"

"Phoebe. Of course. We met socially."

"Do you know of anyone who might have wanted to do harm to Mr Vance?"

For the first time since they had met her, Rose Heath showed real emotion. Tears flooded her eyes, and she reached for a box of tissues. She tore out several and blew her nose, dabbed at the moisture on her cheeks.

"He was well liked. His patients liked him, and his colleagues respected him. Why would anyone want to harm him?"

"That's what we need to find out," Jordan said.

He asked whether there were disgruntled patients, someone unhappy with their treatment, or the facilities in the clinics. Rose insisted that she knew of nothing like that. High on her agenda was making them understand just how wonderful the clinic was and that nobody could possibly find fault with it.

Jordan was aware of Stella huffing and giving the occasional quiet snort. He knew she would have a lot to say when the interview was over.

He tried again to pin down just where the matron had been, eventually suggesting she show them her passport and tickets. The passport was in her briefcase upstairs or maybe in her handbag, she wasn't sure, and the tickets had all been on her phone and now deleted. With no warrant and no real reason to request one, Jordan decided they were not going to get anything more of value, but when they left, he had the distinct feeling that there was more that Rose Heath had to tell them.

Chapter 25

They left Wavertree as the evening became dull and overcast. Stella was more than happy to go straight back to Crosby. The thought of Jordan's cosy home, the little boy, and the good food that was always on offer gave them something to look forward to after what had been a frustrating few hours.

"What did you think, boss?" she said.

"Oh, I don't know. I didn't really like her. That's awful and, of course, we don't have to like her, but I felt she was holding something back. Why would that be? Surely her main concern would be to find out who killed her colleague."

He didn't say more because the hands-free phone chirped and a disembodied voice told them that John was calling. He had studied the spreadsheet from Vance's iPad and thought it would be best to go over it together.

"You coming back in, boss?" he said.

Jordan glanced at the clock and at Stella's hopeful face, and invited John to his house as well. Penny wouldn't mind, and they had plenty of food in the freezer. Maybe away from the station, John would relax and they could get a better idea of whatever was troubling him.

Moments after they finished that call, Jane Keene called. She was sending through a report from the lab where Tilly Monk's clothes had been examined. They could tell from her voice that there was something of interest, but she wanted them to read it themselves before it was discussed.

"Shall I call you later?" Jordan said.

"Of course you can, but, actually, I'm off out. Is that okay? Only I've got tickets for a gig and I'm going with my wife."

"Okay," Jordan said. "Is there anything on this that's going to need urgent action?"

"Not really. It's information, and it's a puzzle. I thought you would have some ideas."

"I'll call you in the morning, yes."

"Brill."

"Have a good evening," Jordan said.

"Did you know that, about her?" Stella asked when the call was ended.

"What?"

"That she was gay and married."

"No, I didn't. Does it matter?"

"Not to me, but there's a bloke in records who's been asking about her. I think his nose is going to be put out of joint when I tell him." Stella gave a short laugh.

Chapter 26

By the time John arrived at Jordan's house in Crosby, they were already two drinks ahead of him. An overexcited Harry had insisted Aunty Stella read him his bedtime story and Penny and Jordan were busy in the kitchen reheating pies and preparing vegetables.

"You look tired, love," Penny had said to Jordan, once they were alone.

"No, I'm okay. A bit frustrated, a bit sad, a bit worried, all the usual suspects, but you know the drill. We just have to keep pegging away and it will all come out in the wash. There's extra pressure being watched by the chief constable but I'm not letting that influence me too much, well I'm trying not to. I am sorry about Tilly though. She was doing well the last that I heard. Of course, there was always the chance she would backslide, but…" He shrugged.

"She didn't though, did she? From what you've told me, she was doing okay."

"That's how it seemed, but if she was doing okay then what got her killed?"

There was no answer she could give him, and Penny stepped forward to wrap him in her arms just as Stella walked into the kitchen.

"Oh, do you guys want some privacy?" Stella said.

"Behave," Jordan said. "I'm just having a hug with my lovely wife. You're only jealous."

"No, I'm not." Stella gave Penny a hug. "See, no need for jealousy."

The atmosphere was warm and friendly. It took a while but, with a couple of bottles of beer and some steak pie inside him, John relaxed and unwound.

They brought him up to speed with the interview in Wavertree and as they spoke, the report arrived from Jane Keene. Jordan read it and gave the others a precis.

"They've been through the CCTV on the train and watched Tilly all the way from Central Station. She doesn't meet anyone, doesn't interact with anyone except the ticket inspector, and then when she alights in Ormskirk she leaves the station alone. Of the passengers who travel all the way there, they are mostly groups, couples, mums with prams and what have you. There were a couple of blokes on their own who did the whole journey and Jane has someone trawling camera footage to see if they can track their route afterwards. Of course, once out of the town centre they effectively vanish and anyway, they could be totally innocent. She says that the next bit is more interesting."

Jordan leaned nearer to the screen.

"You still not been to the opticians, boss?" Stella said.

"No, I will." As he spoke, Jordan glanced at his wife, who had crossed her arms over her chest and was watching him with her eyebrows raised. "What! I've said I'll go."

Penny sniffed and turned away to begin slicing a chocolate tart.

He read in silence for a while and then turned the laptop around so that the others could see the image.

"Right, pictures of Tilly's boots." He hovered the tiny white arrow over a stain. "That, on the edge of her heel, that's blood. Not a surprise given the condition of her body you would think, but it's not her blood."

"Could very well be the attacker's," Stella said. "That'll be a big help when we catch them."

"It could be," Jordan said, "but this is even more interesting, I think. See the grass caught in the teeth of the zip?" He pointed with the curser. "That is apparently not grass from the park. It's a different sort and the grass in the park had just been cut and this clump hadn't."

"So, she'd been walking in the grass elsewhere," John said.

"Yes, and there's no grass on the route she took through the town. Not that she was seen to walk on anyway."

Jordan leaned back in the chair and they sat in silence. They all realised that this was potentially important and why. He watched the faces of John and Stella as they reached the same conclusion as himself.

In her message, Jane Keen told them she had arranged for samples to be sent to the technician who was dealing with the murder on Rodney Street.

"She's good, isn't she?" Stella said.

Jordan agreed she was and acknowledged that it seemed they were all on the same page. It was far too early to draw conclusions, but things were coming together. The chocolate tart was delicious, but of the four at the table, only Penny was focused on dessert.

Once the meal was over, Penny excused herself to work in the office. The three detectives opened their tablet computers on the dining table and read the report from West Lancashire in more details. There were already appeals out for information from any of the passengers that travelled on the same train from Liverpool. They had a couple of pictures of Tilly from the journey and the station, and another of her walking through the middle of the town.

Stella agreed readily when Jordan asked her to stay so that he could offer her more to drink and they could travel together the next day to the town centre. John took a little more persuading. At first, he insisted he needed to go home to Skelmersdale, but when they heard the rain pounding on the windows and Jordan pulled a bottle of rum from the cupboard, he nodded.

"Go on then," he said. "I'll just call my dad, so he doesn't worry." He noticed Stella's grin. "It's not what you think." As he spoke, his voice cracked, and he covered his eyes with his hand.

"Sorry, mate. I didn't mean anything. I was just being soft. You know me," Stella said.

"I know. Okay, here's the thing." And in just a few words, he explained why he had been distracted and just what was worrying him.

Chapter 27

John gave them a full his rundown of the health crisis his father was facing, his voice low and depressed, and at one stage he wiped at his eyes. Stella leaned to touch his arm, and he dredged up a smile for her.

"At first, we just thought he'd got a virus or something. Then he had to wait forever for an appointment with the GP. Then he was referred to a consultant and that appointment was cancelled twice." He paused and took a swig of this drink. "Then there were tests, and it all took time. While he was waiting, he just got worse and worse. In the end I was so sick of all the delays I went down the private route. He was livid. He believes in the Health Service. But he was deteriorating in front of me. It's all so bloody pricey though. I've emptied my savings and given back word on a car I had ordered. I can't tell him that. He'd be so upset. Anyway, top and bottom of it, and I'm sorry, boss. I've been doing some shifts in town."

"What sort of shifts?" Jordan said.

"Couple of clubs. Doorman."

"You've been working as a bouncer?" Stella said. "Mate, you must be whacked."

"Yeah, you could say that. Trouble is, I've been taking my dad to all his appointments as well. It's so bloody difficult." He shook his head and took a swig of the rum. "He's all I've got. Just him and me since Mum died. I don't know what I'll do if I lose him."

For a few minutes, nobody spoke.

"Why didn't you say something before now?" Jordan said. "We could have helped. I haven't got much but if a loan will ease things for now…"

"No, mate. No," John said. "I can't ask you to do that."

"You didn't ask me to. I just offered. Not only that, we're family – not just me, but all of us in the force. I'll bet if you let this be known, you'd be inundated with offers. Crowdfunding and all of that."

"Bloody hell, mate," Stella interrupted. "You know you should have come to me and I'd be good for it. Shit, I've got more than enough. I'd give it to you. Not a loan, a gift. What good is my money if I can't do that?"

"I know you would, and that's why I couldn't ask. My da would flay me alive. If he had the strength." He forced out a laugh. "No, he's never asked for anything all his life. Never claimed any benefits or borrowed from anyone. He wouldn't even get a car loan; he saved up for his clapped-out old Vauxhall. He's proud. We have to do it ourselves. Anyway, he's going into hospital. He's back with the Health Service now. I've got the GP on my side a bit. I'm worried sick though. It's not looking good."

The atmosphere had changed, and it wasn't long before they called it a night.

John asked them to keep the problem to themselves, but Jordan insisted he notify HR and the DCI in case there was a need for him to take time off.

"Best thing for me now is to keep busy," John told him. "Da is in good hands and once we have all the tests finished maybe they can start to treat him. Let me just keep working. I've got a loan from the bank. He'd be furious but at least I've been able to cut back on the bouncer shifts. I'll sort it, boss. I will."

Because of the situation, they hadn't had the chance to review the spreadsheet and so, after breakfast on Sunday morning, they gathered around the dining table again and printed out the documents to look at it together.

Much of it was fairly obvious. On one sheet, there were columns that plainly held dates stretching back over two years. Then alongside those, John pointed to a column of initials.

"I've checked this and it's a list of airports, the codes they use. One side is mainly John Lennon EGGP, the others are various places in Europe."

"I don't see anything that could be actual flight times," Stella said.

"No, I agree. I need to investigate the schedules of the airports. I haven't had time to do that yet. From what I see, we have dates, origination, and destination. It shouldn't be too difficult to find out which carrier was flying those routes and whether they were passenger flights or cargo. When I've done that, we have to get the manifests. I haven't reached any firm conclusions here, which is why I haven't asked for a warrant application as yet. I can't even begin to work out what it all means. Why would Vance have a list of air flights? I just can't come up with an explanation."

"It's good work, though, John," said Jordan. "But what about the last couple of columns?"

John shook his head. "No idea. Just letters. Some are repeated often, but I have no idea what they mean. The last column is obviously a record of achievements or successes – well, ticks and crosses, so that's my assumption. Many more ticks, but where there are crosses, there is more code in the next column. Obviously, a cross required some sort of extra input."

The best thing they came up with was to send their thoughts to the rest of the team and just ask for any and all ideas.

"Of course," Jordan said. "We don't know how important this is and what bearing it could have on Vance's murder, but it's odd. I'm thinking we may need to speak to Mrs Vance and maybe the matron, and the clinic manager perhaps. But we'll hold that for now. It was hidden and we don't know who from. We don't want to play our hand and alert someone to the fact that we know about it. Ha, not that we understand much of it yet."

* * *

Once the visitors had headed off, Jordan and Penny took their son for a walk on the beach. It was bright and sunny. The river sparkled and there were boats in the estuary. For a short while, Jordan unwound and tried to clear his mind, but the things that didn't quite fit were a constant niggle.

Back home, he reviewed the report from Jane Keene and sent a message to Vickie Frost. He didn't expect a response, but an email pinged within a few minutes. She confirmed what he had already surmised and ended the email with a thumbs up emoji and a trophy cup.

He left Penny, who was snoozing on the settee while Harry had his nap, and drove into the city to put his findings on the board ready for the status meeting in the morning, and he sent a message to Josh Lewis to give him something to present to the gold team. It didn't give them any clear answers, but at least there were now more questions and that was good in its own way.

Chapter 28

As Jordan took his place beside his desk, the Monday morning chatter fizzled out and the team waited quietly. He knew they'd all reviewed the notes he'd added and reached the same conclusion. It had also been confirmed in the email from Vickie Frost. The grass in the zipper of Tilly's boot was an excellent match for the grass in the back garden of the clinic. It would be a while before they had the results back from the blood samples, but there was little doubt that it would turn out to be the same blood that had been spread across the floor of the landing and tracked down the fire escape of the clinic on Rodney Street.

The only likely explanation was that Tilly had been at the crime scene. Whether she was involved in the murder was something they could only speculate about, and he cautioned them yet again about jumping to conclusions.

"We'll wait for confirmation about the blood and then revisit this," he said. "Stella is chasing the lab, so fingers crossed for a quick turnaround."

They still had not found the murder weapon in Ormskirk and after the second killing, the search for it in Liverpool had been scaled back.

"In the meantime," Jordan continued, "let's work on thoughts about this spreadsheet. John's done a lot of the work, but now we need some new ideas."

A few of the clerks had printed out the spreadsheet and others were looking at it on their screens. There was a quiet hum with the occasional burst of laughter or ribbing at some of the more outrageous suggestions. It was good; even the unlikely suggestions could lead somewhere.

Sharon Taylor joined Jordan at the table by the window where he was pouring coffee. He glanced at her and raised his eyebrows.

"I was talking to the girls in town last night. Suze and Lena, you remember?" she asked.

He nodded.

"Well, I've been thinking about Tilly and how she was searching for her mate, Brenda. I expect everyone has, but anyway, it was on my mind. So, I did a bit of digging using the name that Suze gave us and I reckon I found her. Turns out she'd known Tilly for a while. I think they met on the streets. They were picked up in a couple of sweeps, just girls in the same world really, and had similar experiences with drugs and whatnot. They both went through the courts and were recommended for help with their addiction. Thing is though – and this came out of the blue, to be honest, and it might be nothing. I just thought I'd mention it…"

Jordan wished she'd get to the point. He was going to have to stop her rambling when she was relaying information. Not now, though, not when she was in full flow.

"I just had a look at the details about the place Brenda was in. It's run as a charity. It's some sort of rehabilitation centre for recovering addicts. Not like a posh rehab like the celebs go to, I don't think. It's more basic but there's a board of trustees and all of that."

"Yes."

"I was gobsmacked. I suppose I shouldn't really have been when you think about it, but, well, you'll never guess what I found."

"No, I probably wouldn't."

"Look at this." She held up her phone.

He took it from her, peered at the screen, and swiped his fingers over it to zoom in. He heard a snort of laughter beside him as Stella poured herself coffee, muttering 'shoulda gone to Specsavers' under her breath.

The comment he was going to make about respect for senior officers was bitten off as he read the list of names. He held the phone out to his sergeant.

"Bloody hell!" she said.

It was the response he'd expected and it echoed his own feelings entirely.

"Well done, Shas," Stella said. "We've now got our link between Mr Vance and Tilly Monk. Girl, you deserve a pat on the back. Here, have a custard cream." And she held out a biscuit to the other woman, who was blushing furiously.

Chapter 29

It was logical that Sharon would accompany Jordan when he went to visit the hostel for recovering addicts, and it was only fair, as she had discovered the link between Tilly and Vance. They hadn't been in the car long before he regretted the decision to leave Stella in the office. He tried tasking the DC with issuing directions from his *A–Z*, but in no time, she had programmed his sat nav.

"I could give you directions, if you want, but I think I could be just reviewing what we have instead," she said.

He held out the hope of her studying her tablet computer quietly. Actually, she gave a running commentary on all aspects.

The girl had been on the game, she told him. A drug and substance misuser who had been done for shoplifting. There followed a list of shops and the names of the officers involved. By this time, Jordan was biting his tongue. He realised she was nervous, and a little intimidated being with him and he didn't want to make matters worse, but when she began on a list of the articles stolen, he had no choice but to interrupt and suggest she focus more on the details of Brenda's time in the hostel.

"Oh, yeah," said Sharon. "So, it was after the last time she was in court. About three weeks later." She read out the dates.

To Jordan's immense relief, the robot voice told them they had reached their destination, and Sharon was out of the car before he had switched off the engine.

The smoking shelter was located near the front door but a small group of residents had chosen not to walk the extra few steps that would have taken them a little way from the entrance. Jordan asked one of them for the manager and the short, wiry bloke gestured with a thumb over his shoulder to the double doors, moved slightly to one side and then hunched back into his padded jacket.

They had both been to similar establishments in the past. The smell of stale bodies and cheap food, pizza, noodles, and chips argued with a hint of disinfectant and cigarette smoke. There was a sectioned off area in the hallway forming a small office. Noticeboards held information regarding group sessions, helplines, and the total ban on smoking in the common areas. The small office was empty. Jordan led Sharon along a narrow, blue-painted corridor. Many of the doors were closed. There was the low rumble of televisions and music, and the zings and twangs of computer games.

Still no sign of a member of staff.

A door at the furthest end of the corridor stood open and a bleak light shone through from inside. There was the noise of yet another television, but above that were raised voices, words tumbling and jousting.

Jordan stepped in front of Sharon and pushed the door open wider. A couple of figures leaning against the wall glanced at them. But the main activity centred around a second group, bending over a figure curled into the seat of a small sofa. One of this gathering turned and glared at them.

Jordan took out his warrant card and held it up in front of him.

"Got our hands full just now, mate. If you're not here to help, wait by the office or bugger off. I'll see you when I've sorted this mess."

There was no option. Jordan and Sharon turned away to find a small figure behind them. The young woman, dressed in a hoody and jeans, stared at them, her eyes huge and frightened. It was impossible for Jordan to push past and head back down the narrow space.

He smiled at the girl. "Hello, are you okay?"

She shook her head as tears flooded from her eyes, and she wiped them away with the sleeves of her top that were pulled down to cover all but the tips of her fingers.

"Is she alright?" she asked, pointing into the room and the group of people around the settee.

"I'm sure she is," Jordan said.

"There's blood."

Jordan glanced at Sharon, who widened her eyes and grimaced. "Where's the blood?" Jordan said.

"On her door." The young woman pointed again at the figure who was the centre of attention. "She's a fucking div. Greg'll have her for this. She's really in trouble now."

"Show me where this blood is," Jordan said.

They followed the girl back along the corridor to where one of the doors stood ajar. There was a smear of red around the handle and a couple of drops on the carpet tiles. Jordan made his way inside to find an empty room. There was a T-shirt on the floor stained with blood, but no sign of any other injured people.

"Stupid cow," the girl said. "I expect they'll have to take her to the ozzy now. Wouldn't want to be her when they bring her back."

From what they'd seen, the situation was being dealt with. If there was a need for police involvement, there'd be time enough when calm had been restored. In the interim, the best thing would be to help the girl in front of them.

"Do you want a cup of tea or coffee?" Jordan said. "We can make you one if you like. We can sit down and talk." It was possible he was overstepping a line somewhere, but it was unthinkable to turn away.

"I'll show you the kitchen. Will yous have a brew with me?"

"Yeah, of course we will. What's your name?" Sharon said.

The girl shook her head. "Doesn't matter."

"Is it your friend that's hurt herself?" Sharon asked.

"Daft bitch. They were going to be chucking her out next week. Bet they'll still make her go down the flats."

Chapter 30

While Sharon made coffee, Jordan sat with the young woman who was still unwilling to share her name. Jordan introduced himself and the PC and she was unfazed by the fact that they were police.

"There's biccies in that tin. You can have one if you want, only don't let Greg know."

For a short while, they sipped the drinks and listened to the back and forth of footsteps in the corridor outside. The flash of blue lights told them that an ambulance had been called and the flurry of activity beyond the door could only have been the entry of paramedics. The elevation in the noise level suggested some of the smokers from outside had come in to find out what was happening. A uniformed officer opened the door. Jordan showed him his ID.

"We came with the ambulance. They didn't tell us somebody was already here," the bobby said.

"We're here about something else," Jordan said. "Just a coincidence. If you need any help, let us know."

"Nah – you're sound, sir. They're taking her to get stitched up. Not much to worry about; poor thing's in a bit of a state, but we've got this."

Sharon leaned closer to the girl. "So, how long have you been here?" she asked.

The response was a shrug.

They sat and sipped at the drinks until the fuss outside quieted and the blue lights faded into the distance.

"Do you know what happened to your friend?" Jordan said.

"What friend?"

"The injured woman."

"Who said she was my friend? She's a daft mare."

"Okay. So, do you know what happened to her?"

"Cut herself, probs. Done it before. Thinks it'll mean they'll keep her. She was supposed to be finished here next week."

"You said. Do you know why she'd want to stay? I mean, it's okay, but surely you all want to leave. When you're strong enough, of course?" Sharon said.

The look that was thrown across the table carried a mixture of scorn and something that could be pity. "D'ya reckon? Shows just what you know."

"So how could they send her away, then?" Jordan said, though he knew he sounded naïve and out of touch. He was fully aware that this sort of place was better than the streets or back to a place where the threat of violence was all that was waiting. But he wanted the woman to talk.

The girl shrugged and pulled her hood up over her head. She wrapped her arms around herself and lowered her face toward her knees. "You've gotta go now," she said. "Greg'll be looking for you. The ambulance is gone. He'll get a right cob on if he finds you in here."

As if she had conjured him up, the door slammed open and the big man from the room at the end of the corridor appeared in the doorway.

"Christ," said Greg, "are you kidding me? You're taking the piss, aren't you?"

Jordan stood and walked towards him, his hand out, and Greg reluctantly grasped it.

"This young woman was upset," said Jordan. "We saw you were involved in handling the incident and thought we'd keep out of your way. You should have been informed that we were coming."

"Yeah, some woman rang, but that was before things went tits up. Look, come into my office." He picked up the biscuit tin, took out one to stuff into his mouth and then put it back in the cupboard. "You should go back to your room, Angie. I don't know what you think you're doing in here. They've put a film on in the lounge if you want company." He nodded at Jordan. "Like I said, best if you come to my office." With that, he stomped from the room.

In Greg's office, he made much of searching for a file, which he pulled from a grey cabinet in the corner of the small room. Any hope that it might be relevant to their visit was quashed when he opened the door and waved it in the air to be collected by a short woman identified as a staff member by the lanyard round her neck and the specks of blood on the front of her blouse.

"Make some copies of her reports. There'll be an inquiry, so be best if we get ahead of things."

The attempt to show who was running things was boring and familiar, but Jordan gave this man his moment to keep him on their side. When Greg sat back behind his desk and folded his hands on top of the notebook in front of him, Jordan summoned up a smile. Sharon took out her notebook, opened it and pulled out a pen. She earned Brownie points for being aware of the power play and the attempt to swing things back to them.

"We're looking for information about one of your ex-residents," Jordan said. "We have a first name, Brenda, and Baxter as a surname. We really need to trace her and anything you can tell us will be a great help."

"Doubt it."

"Sorry?" Jordan said.

"Not going to be much help because I can't tell you bugger all. You should know that. No, mate, bring me a warrant and I'll see what I can do, but coming in here expecting me to talk about our clients, you need to give your head a wobble."

"I had hoped we could move things more quickly," Jordan said. "It could be a matter of life and death. One woman has already been killed and it's possible there is a connection to a second murder. So, you can see we really need to speak to anyone who might have information that will help."

"Nope. No can do. Get a warrant, end of."

Sharon had been writing in her notebook, and both men were taken aback when she spoke.

"Where are the flats?" she asked.

Greg blinked. "What?"

"The flats. Angie said that the girl who cut herself would be going to the flats."

"I've got nothing more to say. There's a lot to do now to get things back under control. The residents are going to be hyper. We've got a tricky night ahead of us. I want you to leave and don't come back without paperwork, yeah?" He stood and gestured towards the door. They had no choice.

* * *

It was late when they left the hostel. "These flats then?" Sharon said. "That's odd, isn't it?"

"How so?"

"Well, the hostel's for looking after them. Then when they've got themselves sorted, they just fling 'em out. That's what happened to Lena. That's when she met Suze, and thank God she did because I don't know what would have happened if…"

Jordan coughed.

"Sorry, boss. I go on too much, don't I?"

"A bit, yes. But go back to your thoughts about the flats. You need to try to stick to facts, you know, when it's to do with the job."

"Yeah, I know. I've always been the same. Me mam says I can talk for England, but I don't know where she's coming from. You should hear her gabbing on."

Jordan coughed again. They both laughed. "The flats," he said.

"Yeah, so, maybe it's something else the charity does. You know, a sort of halfway house thing. That's dead nice if it is, and it might help us find Brenda."

"Yes, it's a good thought. So, first we have to find out what the deal is and where this accommodation is located. Our Greg there wasn't a lot of help, but I guess we can't criticise him for sticking to the rules. Well, we can, but it won't get us anywhere."

"Yeah, but I bet if he wanted something, the rules wouldn't matter so much. I think that Angie was scared of him," Sharon said.

"Paranoia, I think that goes along with drug misuse."

"You could be right, but I didn't like him much. Is it okay if I do a bit of a background check?"

"Of course. But I reckon that's already been done for him to be working there. It's a tough job, but there's no harm in looking."

"I expect you're right. I'll just have a scan, though. Anyway, the flats," Sharon said.

Jordan frowned and took a deep breath. "Okay. So, the link with Tilly and Vance is through the hostel. She was there, and he is on the board. So, is the hostel attached to the clinic via their charity work? Then the flats, how do they fit in? From what we've just heard, they are connected to the hostel. We need to clarify all the connections. Maybe the best thing will be to talk to the matron. Set that up for tomorrow in the morning. Do you want me to drop you off at home?"

"No, back in town'll be great. I'm out on the lash with some mates."

"Okay, but I want you in bright and early in the morning."

"Yeah, no probs. I'll be there. Shall I meet you at the office or at the matron's place?"

"The office. We should have a catch-up with the rest of the team first."

Chapter 31

It was dark with only a hint of moonlight. The duck pond was a black mirror pecked with the glow of streetlights from the main road. Bushes shivered in the wind; shadowed branches rustling and scratching together. There was an unlikely owl somewhere and the church clock chimed. As it finished, there was a pause, still and silent until a cat passed low to the ground, with something small in its jaws, a dead or dying thing or just pickings from the rubbish bin. It was impossible to tell.

In the corner where it had happened, there was still police tape and a couple of cans left by rubberneckers who had come with phones and gone away disappointed. Nothing to see, all hidden. The filth shifting the good stuff. But he knew what had been there. He closed his eyes and replayed the moment the girl had crumpled at his feet. He felt a stirring when he remembered the blood pooling in the grass and the strange rattle of her breath in the last minutes until it was over.

It had been better than the first time. He'd been too nervous then. The setting had been too ordinary, just a building, furniture, and the bloke too ordinary in his suit and tie. It wasn't his choice. But, the girl, slight and willowy, like a wraith, yes, that was the right word, like someone not made of flesh and bone. It had been good. Just what he was looking for. Unreal.

When he did it again, it had to be outside, in the dark. It would take organising, but he could do it. He was the one in charge; he had the power.

He bent a little at the knees, braced and held his arm out in front of him, one hand grasping the imaginary weapon. No, wait. He scanned the ground – nothing, and so he broke a branch from one of the bushes. Now he crouched again and began the movements. It was perfect; he had practiced so many times he was perfect. He had the power.

It probably wouldn't be around here, though. He could go wherever he wanted to, and why would he make do with this shitty little place. No, back in the city, part of the buzz. There was the money from the first job, enough to rent somewhere. Once that was in the account, he was going to be free of them all, his own man. That had been the only downside with the girl. He wouldn't ever be paid. But it had been necessary and, in the end, just what he had hoped for and more. When she'd appeared on top of that fire escape at the clinic, he'd nearly shit himself. Thought it was a disaster. Yeah, he'd panicked, for a minute, what with her screaming and all. Stupid, nosey cow, but he showed her, didn't he. He showed her good and proper.

Chapter 32

True to her word, Sharon was in with the rest of the team for the status meeting at seven on Tuesday morning. Her eyes were red-rimmed, and she had a huge cardboard cup of coffee in her hands but she was on the ball when Jordan asked her to give everyone a rundown on the visit to the hostel. She strayed from the main narrative a couple of times, but a cough from Jordan saw her back on track.

It was disturbing that most of the tasks assigned afterwards were simply going over witness statements again, looking for something they might have missed. There was hardly anything new coming in. No sightings or information from the appeal in Ormskirk and, with almost a week gone, there had been nothing from the visitors to the buildings in Rodney Steet. If they didn't have some new information soon, the case would go cold. That couldn't happen; two people had had their lives stolen, and they deserved justice.

Sharon was supposed to accompany Jordan on his visit to see the matron, but she was now slumped in her desk chair, scrolling through reports on her computer. He'd given her a warning about burning the candle at both ends, but it wouldn't do anyone any harm to be sympathetic to her delicate state and, really, he wanted Stella with him.

While Jordan was in his office collecting his jacket and car keys, Stella made a call to confirm the meeting with Rose Heath. As he turned to leave, John knocked on the door frame.

"Alright, John. First of all, how's your dad doing?"

"I dropped him off for a scan earlier. It's just a waiting game, to be honest. He seems to be going down the nick though. It's horrible to see."

"I'm sorry. Anything I can do, just let me know."

"Thanks. I've just had a call, boss. It's an odd one, but it must mean something."

"Okay."

"It's about that patient, the Griffith woman."

Jordan perched on the edge of his desk as John gave him a quick round-up of the facts. The control room had patched through a call from a member of staff aboard the cruise ship. They had made landfall for a visit to Gran Canaria and a nighttime visit to Las Palmas. There was to be dinner and entertainment. It was all routine stuff. The Griffiths had gone ashore, but when the tour coach had returned in the early hours, they were not with the group. The crew had made a search for them and called their mobiles repeatedly but had been unable to contact them. That they had been spoken to by the police earlier was a matter of record and once the staff captain was told of their disappearance, he had wasted no time letting the police know just what was going on.

"Okay, contact the ship. I want their rooms searched. We're concerned about their welfare, so we don't need a warrant. Any kick-back, let me know. I assume they have a steward who was in there regularly, so it won't take much for them to assess the situation. Find out if they took their passports. From what little I know, I think there are specific cruise cards for when passengers go ashore in an organised group – check that, will you. If they have taken other ID, that could give us an idea of whether this was intentional or some sort of mishap that caused them to miss the coach back. Strange that no-one has been in touch, if it was an accident or something like that. John, keep me informed and I guess we'd better find out who we need to contact in the local police and port authorities."

"I asked about the passports," said John, "they have a safe in the cabin. It's where most passengers keep their documents and whatnot. I've asked for it to be opened and they were sorting that. Do you want me to reach out to the locals?"

"Not yet. They've not been missing long. Wait until we hear back from the ship. Try to call Mr and Mrs Griffith on their mobiles. Though I guess that's going to be a non-starter. Organise a BOLO for airports and ports. It could be simply that they wanted to come home, but I very much doubt it. No, this is bloody suspicious. Get on it."

As John left the office, Jordan grabbed his jacket and went to meet Stella who confirmed that the matron was at the clinic and had been less than pleased to know that they were on the way to speak to her. "She was proper snide – sorry, boss, but she was. All *'I don't have time'* and *'make an appointment'*. Anyway, I got just as snotty and left her no option."

* * *

The smell of paint hit them as they stepped through the door on Rodney Street. The staircase and hallway were draped with drop cloths and on the landing, someone was whistling among the clatter of tins and equipment. Vivienne Campbell, the clinic manager, greeted them at the reception desk and took them to Rose Heath's office. They were offered coffee, and partly because of the irritated expression on the matron's face, Stella accepted.

"I'm very busy. I can only give you a couple of minutes. You can see the state that we're in. We're having to decorate everywhere."

"Where are you seeing patients?" Jordan asked.

"Out in Aughton at the inpatient clinic. We're having to ferry people in cars. You can imagine what that's doing to costs."

"You don't see people at the hostel, then?"

There was silence for a moment before the matron snapped at them. "Don't be ridiculous. Our patients could never be subjected to that place."

"So, you don't consider the residents there your patients?" Jordan said.

"No. Well, not in the same way. We occasionally arrange treatment if they need urgent care, but there is a staff of therapists on site to help with their ongoing recovery. It's not part of the group."

"What happens once they're clean and sober?" Stella said.

"They move on."

"On to where?"

"It depends."

"What does it depend on?" Stella said.

"Their situation. I thought you came to talk about Mr Vance and his horrible murder. It had nothing to do with the hostel."

"Didn't it?" Jordan said.

For a moment, the woman just frowned at them. "No, of course it didn't. It's a separate thing altogether. How could it possibly be connected?"

"We have to look at all possibilities. How often did Mr Vance visit the hostel?" Jordan said.

"He didn't. Well, occasionally if there was a special event. There is a summer fete to raise funds and a Christmas lunch. He shows his face at those, of course, but he doesn't go in the normal way of things. Why on earth would he? He was interested in what was done there but it's not part of his clinic responsibilities, it's charity work, separate. You do understand what that is, don't you?"

"And you?"

"Me?"

They waited in silence again. The matron had retreated behind her desk and picked up a pen, which she used to make a note on a pad.

"Yes, do you visit the hostel?"

"I do sometimes, yes. It looks good in the reports to head office. Shows we are genuinely interested in the charity side of things, helping those less fortunate."

"And the flats?" Jordan said.

"Flats?" Rose jotted a couple more notes on the pad and bent to lift her bag from where it sat on the floor, rooted through it and then refastened it and dropped it back where it had been.

Jordan asked again and leaned forward, forcing her to look at him. "The flats that some of the residents go to when they are discharged. Where are they?"

"It's irrelevant. Mr Vance would never have been there. Look, I have to get on. I don't have time to spend with you and I don't want to answer any more of your questions. I think you should leave now."

She stood and ushered them out of the room. There was no point trying to carry on.

"Well, that was interesting," Stella said.

Chapter 33

"What next, boss?" Stella asked.

They had walked from the police station to Rodney Street and now took the quickest way back along Seymour Street. As they were passing the terrace of houses opposite the big red-brick building housing a gym and offices, Jordan's phone rang. They crossed to the grassy patch on the other side of the road to shelter in the empty bus stop so that they could listen on speaker. John's voice, lively and animated, told them that the steward had accessed the Griffiths' cabin.

"I spoke to him directly. He went in with the security bods and they found the safe unlocked and empty of all documents and of the jewellery he had seen Pauline Griffith wearing. There were clothes in the wardrobe, but the designer handbag that he had noticed previously was also missing. Dave, the steward – actually, he calls himself a cabin attendant – seems to know a lot about handbags. Anyway, he reckons it's worth a couple of grand and apart from that, there were no cufflinks or any of that stuff that he was used to seeing on the dresser. Basically, they took anything of value."

"I'm coming straight back to speak to the DCI," Jordan said. "We need to contact the local police in Las Palmas. At the moment, all we can say is that we need to speak to these people. We don't have anything except that this is odd behaviour, and they are witnesses to a major crime – well, one of them is. I just don't know about him now. We need access to phone records. We'll be back in a few minutes now."

John came to meet them before they had even taken off their coats. He was grinning and looked more alive than he had for weeks.

"D'ya reckon we might have got them, boss? I mean, it's odd, isn't it? They've been involved from the start, knew the Vances before, and now this. Be a real result if we've got them so quickly."

Jordan shook his head. "It's something, John, that's for certain, but I reckon we have to keep it in perspective. But the main kicker with this is Tilly."

"How do you mean?"

"Let's suppose the Griffiths were the ones who killed Roland Vance. After that, there was another killing with a similar or the same weapon, and as near as possible, the same strike pattern. Are you with me?"

John frowned and nodded.

"Well," Jordan continued, "when Tilly was seen on CCTV in Ormskirk, the Griffiths were on the high seas. That would mean we have two completely separate murderers. It's not impossible. We know that life throws up weird coincidences all the time, but there are too many things pointing to the same killer. There's the blood on Tilly's shoe, the similarity of the wounds, all of that. They were both really nasty, violent killing. I don't think I can see Frederick Griffith slashing away with a zombie knife. He's a middle-aged bloke, running to seed a bit. This crime took some strength and, I hate to say this but, some skill. Wielding a weapon like that, it's not easy. As I say, it's not impossible but, no, I'm not convinced."

John's shoulders slumped.

Jordan put a hand on his arm. "Print me a record of the interview we had with them, plus the original statement from her."

"What's going on, boss?" Stella asked.

Jordan shook his head. "Just an idea, but I don't want to voice it yet. It could likely be nothing, but it was more his attitude than anything. Anyway, with them disappearing, I'm going to speak to DCI Trent. We should get a warrant to search the Griffiths' house."

Chapter 34

The atmosphere in the office was charged. There had been elation when it seemed that there had been a major development and that was now subdued by the news that the boss was far from convinced.

Sharon met Jordan as he was making coffee. "Ha. We'll have to stop meeting like this, boss," she said.

Jordan raised his eyebrows and pursed his lips.

She blushed. "Sorry. Inappropriate, I get it. I just thought you'd want to know. Suze has called."

Jordan nodded.

"Yeah, well, that Brenda has been hanging around. They reckon she's in a squat down near the cathedral."

"When did they see her?"

"Well, Suze just called me and I was in the bog. I don't like answering the phone in there, so I had to call her back and…"

"When, PC Taylor?"

"Just now, boss. I mean, she saw her just now and said she was in a bit of a state, and she was going back to the squat in the Mews."

"And you know where that is?"

"Yes, boss. I got the address from Suze. Not that she's staying there."

"Send the address through to my phone. Now."

As he left Sharon, wide-eyed and befuddled, Jordan called to Stella to meet him outside immediately.

* * *

They were surprised by the squat. It wasn't an old, damp shambles as they had assumed, but part of a three-sided terrace of flats built of red brick with fenced-off gardens planted with trees and shrubs. A dog tethered to a metal stake driven into the ground acted as a very efficient sentry, setting up a cacophony of barking as soon as Jordan and Stella stepped into the garden. Stella stopped and Jordan glanced back to see her shaking her head.

"Don't like dogs, boss. He's a big one."

"It's okay," said Jordan. "He's tied up and see, he's not sure about us. He's backing away."

"Don't care. What if he's just gearing up to pounce?"

"My nana always said barking dogs don't bite," Jordan said.

"Aye well, why not call your nana and get her to go past him?"

A tall, slender man dressed in jeans and a long shirt covered by a leather waistcoat stepped around the side of the block. He held up a hand and, with a toss of his head, he quieted the animal that shuffled back into a makeshift kennel wedged against the wall.

"Don't mind Buster," he said. "He's all noise; he's dead soft, really. Can I help you?"

Jordan took out his warrant card and held it in front of him.

The man nodded. "Afternoon. I'm Jez. I see there's just two of you, so I'm assuming you're not here to evict us. If you are, I think you should have a word with the landlord. He knows we're here and is cool with it for the moment. He knows we're keeping the place clean and discouraging vandals. We'll move out next week to give them a chance to get it ready for occupation once the students come back to uni."

"We're looking for a young woman," Jordan said. "If she's around, we just need a word. It's about a serious crime and we've been told she might be here. Brenda? Is there someone here called Brenda?"

Jez didn't speak, he didn't turn away, and he didn't blink. The message was clear.

"Look, mate," Stella said. "She's not in trouble. Not as far as we know. She could be in danger, though. All we want to do here is have a quick word. Her friend's been killed. If she's here, you'll know that. She must have told you. Last we heard, she wasn't doing so well."

Jez bent down to untie the dog. Stella took a couple of steps backwards and slid sideways behind Jordan. The other man grinned and wrapped the rope around his fist. "Stay there." With that, he walked back out of sight.

It wasn't long before Jez came back. "Okay, you'll need to come this way," he said.

He led them to the rear of the building, where a window was open. There was a wooden crate which Jez stepped onto to slide through the gap. He pushed the window wider to allow Jordan to clamber through. Stella waved aside the helping hand the boss offered. She sat on the sill and swung her legs round, dropping lightly to the floor.

"Bren says she'll speak to you," Jez said. "But she wants me with her." He lowered his voice. "She's not too good right now. Be kind, yeah." He stepped aside and ushered them in with a wave of his arm.

"Where's what's-its-name?" Stella said, pointing to the water bowl on the floor.

"I've tied him in the back. You'll be fine."

The door led into a square room. With no lights on, it was dark. On the desk fixed to the wall were a couple of candles in jars, but they weren't lit. It was cold. The room was tidy, though there were a few nylon shoulder bags piled in one corner and a cardboard crate holding beer cans on a shelf beneath the desk. There was a kettle on the floor with a couple of mugs on a plastic tray along with a packet of cheap biscuits and a box of tea with a spoon handle sticking out of the top. Two folding garden chairs faced each other in the middle of the room, and a tall stool with a torn plastic seat was pushed against the wall.

They heard the shuffle of footsteps in the hallway. The door swung back and a small figure wrapped in a thin, stained, coverless duvet moved quietly into the room. The girl took small halting steps towards the chairs and grabbed at the back of the nearest one. Jez reached out and steadied her with one hand on her arm. He helped her to settle herself with the bedding wrapped around her.

"Brenda?" Jordan said.

She nodded and raised her eyes to squint at him. She rubbed a sleeve under her nose, sniffed and pulled the cover closer, gripping it at her throat.

"D'ya fancy a cuppa, queen?" Jez said.

She nodded again and sighed.

"We came to talk about your friend Tilly," Jordan said.

The girl twisted her head to look at him and tears flooded from her red-rimmed eyes.

"You're not well though, Brenda. Maybe this isn't the best time. Maybe we should get you some help. Do you want to see a doctor?" Stella said.

"No." The voice was filled with panic. "Don't want nothing. Just leave me. Jez is looking after me. Aren't you?" As she looked at her friend her chin quivered, and she gulped back tears.

"I am, yes," said Jez, "and you're doing really well." He took a step to stand beside her. "She's not been good since she heard about Tilly. It knocked her sideways a bit, but she's getting better again."

"Maybe we could see about her going back to the hostel," said Stella. "Just for a couple of weeks, until she's stronger?"

It was as if Stella had slapped the girl. Brenda stood up from the chair and tried to reach out to Jez, but her legs and feet tangled in the duvet and the chair, and she fell to the floor with a clatter and a yell. "No, there's no point going back there. They won't let me in and anyway, I don't want to; don't want nothing from them."

All three stepped forward, but Jez was the one who helped her to her feet. He shook out the duvet and wrapped it around Brenda's shoulders. She leaned against him for a moment, and he led her to the chair.

"It's okay. Don't panic. We're not here to make you do anything you don't want to," Jordan said. "All we want to do is talk about Tilly. I knew her; well, I'd met her. She was okay. I liked her. I want to find out what happened. We need to catch who did that awful thing to her. Do you think you know anything that might help us? We've already found out that you two were friends."

"I didn't see her," said Brenda. "We were supposed to meet up, and she was going to help me. She said I could stay with her till she sorted things for me, but then she sent a message to say she'd had to go away and not to tell anyone. I didn't have anywhere to stay. I was scared. She never told me where her place was, so I couldn't go and find her. After that, I don't know what happened. I was in the town, I was out of it a bit, and then Jez found me and brought me here. They killed her, didn't they? It's my fault. I shouldn't have caused a fuss. If I'd known, I wouldn't have never said anything."

None of it made sense. By now, the young woman was sobbing and shaking. Jez stepped forward and put his hand on her shoulder. He shook his head.

Jordan sighed. "We'll come back in a couple of days. Maybe when Brenda's feeling better, we can talk again. If you have to move in the meantime, can you let me know?" Jordan held out a business card.

"Maybe," Jez said.

"Are you sure she shouldn't be in hospital or something?" Stella said.

"No, we'll get her through this. I hope you find out what happened to her friend."

Chapter 35

The drive back to St Anne Street was less than ten minutes and they passed the clinic, which now looked as though nothing untoward had taken place there. They discussed Brenda's outburst on the way, but it was impossible to decipher the garbled words.

"She's doolally right now," Stella said. "Looks as though she's still under the influence of something. All that about not causing a fuss. What the hell does that mean?"

"We'll see her again, maybe later tomorrow. If Jez really is looking after her properly, she might have improved by then. We can't rely on much of what she says at the moment, she's just too sick and scared. In the meantime, John's sent a message." Jordan nodded at his phone in the holder on the dashboard. "We've got a warrant to search the Griffiths' house and access to their phone records."

"We could shoot off there now."

"Yes. Also, I want Kath to contact Mrs Vance in Bath and find out if she's heard from them. I want to know when she's planning on coming back. I don't want to have to go down there if we can help it. It'd take too much time, but we need another word. Sort that, would you?"

"Can we call in at the station, boss? I need a wee and a quick drink."

* * *

While Stella headed for the toilets, Jordan stepped into the office to scrawl a note on the whiteboard with Brenda's current location and the fact that she'd been going to meet Tilly. It felt important, but as yet he couldn't work out why.

Violet Purcell stood in front of the board. As Jordan watched, she peered down at the tablet computer and then back at the board. She nodded and when she turned, she saw him watching. She raised a finger as if she was about to speak.

"You alright there, Vi?" Jordan said.

"I'm good, boss. Sorry, did you want to get in here?" She stepped to one side.

"Do you want to tell me anything?" Jordan was grinning at her, and she smiled back.

"Not right now. I need to double-check a couple of things. But I'm working on something. Hopefully, I'll be able to explain at the next meeting."

"I was thinking we could have a quick one tonight. There's been some movement."

"Ha, movement." With the strange comment, she walked back to her workstation.

There was no sign of John in the office, his computer was logged off and his jacket missing from the back of his chair. When Jordan asked about his whereabouts, nobody had seen him leave and he hadn't told anyone where he was going.

Jordan sent a text asking him to check in and that he and Stella were on their way to the Griffiths' house and he could join them there.

Chapter 36

When they left for Allerton, the sky was overcast and by the time they arrived in the tree-lined cul-de-sac, a dreary drizzle had set in. A red Jaguar was parked on the paved drive, in front of a large brick-built detached house. A glance at the soffits showed security cameras just under the guttering and there was a yellow anti-theft device attached to the steering wheel of the car.

"You'd have thought they'd have put it away if they were leaving it," Stella said. She stepped forward and rang the doorbell. After a couple of moments, she thumped hard with the side of her fist on the highly polished front door. There was no response.

Jordan boosted himself up on the timber gate at the side of the house. "There's a garage, but the entrance is round the corner," he said. "We'll have a look. Chances are it's like mine, full of other stuff. Or maybe they have more cars than they can fit in there. Looking at this place, they're not short of a bob or two. Mind you, we knew that, didn't we?"

"I called the locksmith before we left. I reckoned the place would be empty. I thought he would have been here by now," Stella said.

"We'll hang on a bit longer. I don't want to do any damage if we can help it," Jordan said. "We're still not sure what these two are up and if they've just gone off on a little adventure, we're going to have egg on our faces if they complain to their mate, the chief constable, even though we've got the warrant. What are you doing?"

"These rocks, round the bottom of this tree."

"Yes, all very nice, but why are you ferreting among them?"

"Ferreting?"

"Yeah. Oh, okay, fake rocks. You think there could be a key safe. Bit obvious though, right here on the front."

"Yes, but people are pretty stupid, aren't they? Not these two, though. Not in this case, anyway. These are all just rocks."

"It was a good thought. Try under the plant pots."

"Can I help you?" The voice from the other side of the small hedge was loud and even with so few words, they picked up on the anger.

Jordan pulled out his warrant card and approached the plump older man, who had now moved to the end of the drive. He snatched the small wallet and held it close to his face, glancing up to compare the image with Jordan. He had ignored Stella's outstretched arm and didn't bother to address her.

"So, what are you doing here?" The man glanced up at the drizzling sky and hunched his shoulders. Rain had stuck the sparse strands of hair to his skull, and he pushed a few aside from his brow.

Stella forced him to acknowledge her by stepping in front of him to show him the electronic copy of the warrant on her phone. "We have permission to enter these premises to search. That includes the garden and the garage."

"Well, I can't imagine why you would be doing that, but why don't you come back when Pauline and Fred are in? Surely you don't need to do it now, in the rain."

"It is an urgent matter, sir. We can't wait for the weather to improve," Stella said.

"Well, they might be back later, and we won't have to stand here like idiots, getting soaked."

"There is no need for you to stand there," Stella said.

In response, the man crossed his arms and planted his feet further apart on the wet grass. He tossed his head and stared at her. It was becoming a diversion that would reap no reward.

"How well do you know your neighbours?" Jordan said.

"We're friends. Fred and I play golf." He gestured vaguely toward the nearby golf course. "My wife's dead now, so I don't see as much of Pauline as I used to, but yes, I'd say we were friends."

"And yet, you didn't know they were away," Stella said.

"Of course I did. They went on a cruise. I was surprised to see them back so soon. But Pauline's not been too well, so I just thought she'd come back because she was poorly. Shame that, but Fred will have insurance cover. He's on the ball."

"When did you see them?" Jordan said.

"Last night. I saw the lights on. I thought at first it was just the automatic ones, you know, to confuse burglars, but then I saw them moving about, drawing the curtains and then lights coming on upstairs."

"Well, we still need to get in to have a look. I don't suppose you have a spare key, do you?"

"Yes. But I don't know about this."

"If we can't use a key, then we will have a locksmith open the door and that will inevitably cause damage to the current locks and then we will need to board the entrance. Probably with sheet metal, to deter vandals. It doesn't look very nice, but it works okay. It would be far better if we could just open the door."

As Jordan spoke, a van pulled up to the kerb with the livery of a local locksmith on the side.

The neighbour watched the driver slide out and walk around the back of the van to take out his tool kit.

"Oh, look, just hang on. You'll have it looking like a slum." He pulled a mobile phone from his pocket and dialled. Jordan raised his eyebrows and sighed. They waited quietly for the inevitable and once the man had clicked off the device to abort the unanswered call, he nodded.

"I'll get you the key, but I'll need to come in with you. There's an alarm and no way am I giving you the code, police or not."

It was easier to let him have this small victory than to argue any longer. He stomped into his house and Jordan had a word with the locksmith who let them know that there would still be a bill to pay, key with the neighbour or not. The whole episode was becoming messy and tense. There were two keys, one for a deadbolt and one for a Yale lock. As the locksmith climbed back into his van and slammed the door, the man from next door pushed in front of Jordan to step into the hallway. He turned to the alarm box on the wall and took from his pocket a small card with the numbers printed in large letters. Before he touched the buttons, Jordan stopped him with a raised hand.

"Listen," he said.

Apart from the rattle of rain on the windows and the gurgle of water in the guttering, there was silence. No urgent beeping and no flashing LED.

"That's not like Fred. He's usually very keen on setting the alarm, even if they're only next door with me." The neighbour turned and took a couple of paces towards the open door of the lounge.

"That's fine now; thank you, Mr...?" Jordan said.

"Sweeting, George Sweeting. I'll just check that all is in order."

"No, you won't. Thank you."

Jordan pulled the front door wide and, with a glare, the neighbour stepped out and back onto his own path. He stood for a while watching, but in the end the rain and the chilly wind drove him inside.

They were half expecting the scene that greeted them in the living room. It became obvious very quickly that if the Griffiths had been home, the visit had been very short and frantic or, what was more likely, someone else had pulled out all the drawers from the sideboard and left the roll-fronted desk in a shambles.

Stella was already on the phone calling in the SOC team and then out to the car for shoe covers and gloves before they went any further into the house.

Chapter 37

"I don't suppose the charming neighbour'll be good for a cuppa," Stella said.

"No, I reckon we'll just hang on in the car. I've got a couple of mini Lion bars in the glovebox," Jordan said. "John's been trying to call. I'll ring him back and you can check with the office, see if there's anything else we need to know about and tell the team we'll have a catch-up before the end of shift."

John answered his phone quickly, but his voice was hushed. "Sorry, boss. I had to nip out. I'm at the hospital. Dad's taken a bit of a turn. They're doing tests. Boss, it's not looking good."

"I'm really sorry, John. We'll keep our fingers crossed. Let us know what happens, yeah?"

The SOC team, when they arrived, were disgruntled at a late call, but Vickie Frost was her usual cheerful self. "No blood, no bodies this time, Jordie?"

"No, thank goodness. But someone has been in and had a real good root around. So, evidence of a break-in. It's not a terrible mess, no real damage, but I reckon that whoever came in was more than likely looking for something specific."

"Oh right, so you want me to look for something, but we don't know what it is, and it might already have been nicked?"

"Yeah, that's it. Off you go, Sergeant. Oh, and as soon as possible can I have a copy of the feed from the cameras."

"I'll do what I can, but the cards'll have to go via the technical laboratory."

Back in the car, Stella had found the chocolate and was eating a second small bar. "I hope you left me one," Jordan said when he returned.

"Dunno. But I'm starving. I couldn't resist. They're too small."

Jordan grinned as he took a bar that was hidden in the compartment between the seats. "Penny can't leave them alone. I have to have backup."

"What do you reckon about all this then, boss? I thought she was just a patient, and he was a nowty posh bloke."

"There's something that has bothered me since the interview, and I have been back and forth with it in my head."

"Right, share then."

"When we were speaking to them originally on the ship, the husband made a comment. It was about the clinic. He was protective of his wife and upset about the death of his friend. But he said something about minimising the effect on the business. I've got the exact wording in my report."

"Well, he was, though, wasn't he? Upset about the injuries and that."

"Yes, he was. But how did that relate to the business of the clinic? Wouldn't he be more concerned about the carnage and finding out who did it?"

Stella was silent for a while, staring at the race of raindrops on the windscreen, and then she shrugged. "Well, I guess he's a businessman, and it was just natural to him."

"But he's just been talking about a man being slashed and killed – his words – and then he's all business. It could mean nothing, but it doesn't seem right. All of that makes this" – he waved a hand towards the house – "more suspicious."

"Doesn't really move us on much though, boss."

"No, it doesn't. Now, it looks as though we might lose John for a while. His dad is in a bad way, apparently. I want to go back to the office, have a status meeting, and then why don't you come back home with me tonight and we'll go through everything again without interruption."

* * *

Jane Keene was in the office when they arrived. She was sitting with Violet Purcell, both of them focused on the computer.

Jordan brought everyone up to date on the happenings in Allerton and then assigned tasks asking for all information on the Griffiths, including where their wealth had come from.

"These two are now persons of interest. We need to contact our colleagues in Las Palmas and update them. Sharon, do that and make sure that border control are kept in the loop. If they try to come back into the country, or indeed have already slid past the controls, we need to know. They have a large house here and all that goes with a privileged lifestyle. If they choose to give that up, they must have a damn good reason. Best thing for us, of course, is that they will try to come back home. I've arranged for a patrol to pass regularly for now. We need to know about all their connections with the clinic if there is more than just their friendship with the Vances and Pauline being a patient."

"Like what, boss?" Stella said.

"The charity work with the hostel for instance. Anything really that links them. I also want to know more about these rehabilitation flats and how that all connects. I suppose Brenda Baxter might know more about that and I am planning to have another chat with her soon."

Jordan nodded to Sharon. "Sharon, it's probably a good idea to ask your contacts specifically about that. They might well have an idea."

"When are you going to speak to Brenda again?" Jane said.

"Hopefully tomorrow. Do you want to attend?"

"Yep." As she spoke, she glanced at Stella, who smiled and gave her a discreet thumbs up.

Jordan nodded. "This thing just keeps getting bigger and more complicated, but at least it's movement. That's better than being in the doldrums. So, let's keep at it. Everyone in early tomorrow but get some rest tonight. Stella, seeing as you're now going to be free in the morning, can you phone Mrs Vance and find out when she's expected back from Bath?"

Chapter 38

Penny took one look at her husband and his sergeant and pulled a bottle of red wine from the rack in the kitchen. "Red okay, Stel? I've also got white open or beer?"

"White'd be lovely," said Stella. "Red makes me gloomy sometimes."

"Are you okay?" Penny said.

"Yeah, sound. To be honest, though, we went to a squat today and what with that and the hostel, it's all a bit depressing when the next place was a bloody big gaff in Allerton. It's all so unfair. It makes me feel bad – you know, with my money and that. But take no notice of me. A glass of wine and I'll be fine."

"But you did good with your money. You bought your family homes."

"Well, yeah, but there's so many people in need, isn't there? You know that with your work at the CAB. Then I find out my mate needs money and he won't even ask me. Oh, look, ignore me. I'm just being a miserable cow."

They ate jerk chicken and rainbow rice but didn't drink more wine.

"We'll have a nightcap when we've finished," Jordan said. "Are you staying over?"

"No, I'll shoot off home when we're done here. I've hardly been at my place these last couple of weeks. If I don't get my washing sorted, I'll be wearing pyjamas to the office."

The detectives had just logged on to their tablets, poured coffee, and settled themselves around the table in the dining room when the doorbell rang. They heard

Penny talking in the hall and turned as John Grice appeared in the doorway.

"John, what's to do?" Stella said.

For a minute the DC struggled to speak and then, his eyes sparkling with moisture, he shook his head.

"Me dad," he said. "I've left him in the ozzy."

"Is he having more tests?" Stella said.

"No, he's not." John stopped, gulped and then threw himself on to the nearest chair. He leaned his head on the table for a moment and then looked up and straightened his shoulders. "I shouldn't have come. This isn't your problem. I didn't know where else to go, though. He's got cancer. They've just told us. I suppose I knew already deep down but it's still a gut punch when they put it into words."

"Aw, shit, mate. That's awful," Stella said.

Penny moved into the room and handed John a glass of whisky. She wrapped her arms around his shoulders and lay her cheek against the top of his head. "I am so sorry, John."

John rubbed his eyes. "Well, they're going to start treatment, and we'll have to wait and see but it's pretty advanced and all they can do is try to slow it down. Wouldn't have been, would it, if there hadn't been so many delays? Aw, fuck it." He tossed back the drink and slammed the glass down on the table.

For a while they let him talk and John went through the details and the prognosis.

"Listen, mate. Let me help, we can get him anything. I don't know, maybe send him to America. People do that, don't they, to get the up-to-the-minute treatment?" Stella said.

John sighed and took hold of Stella's hand. "Thanks, love. I really appreciate that, but he won't go for it. I know he won't. Anyway, I got the impression that really there's nothing more anyone can do. No good grasping at straws.

It'll just make it worse in the end. So, it's just a question of time."

The atmosphere was charged. John drank in gloomy silence and Penny poured him more whisky without asking. Stella reached a couple of times to touch his arm as out in the garden a blackbird sang to the deepening evening. After a while, John made moves to leave but they wouldn't let him go. In the end, they got very little work done, and they helped Stella into a taxi as John wobbled upstairs to the spare room in Jordan and Penny's house.

Jordan had controlled his drinking and set the vibrate alarm on his phone early so that by the time John staggered into the kitchen the next morning, Jordan had already spent a couple of hours reviewing what they knew.

"Sorry, boss."

Jordan shook his head, poured them both coffees, and pulled a plate of warm rolls from the oven.

"No need to apologise. I'm glad you felt you could come here. We're all ready to help any way we can, and you should take as much time as you need for hospital visits and whatever you've got to do. I'm sure Stella meant it when she said she'd help out. I understand that you don't want that. But anything, any time. We're here."

"Thanks, boss. I'm just trying to get my head around it. Anyway, he's in the right place for now and I'm ready to get on with the job. There's nothing I can do except visit him and keep him cheerful. Give me tasks, boss. I need to work."

Chapter 39

There were three calls on Jordan's phone by the time he had driven himself and a subdued and overhung John to the town centre. Most of the team were already in the incident room, and the atmosphere was upbeat and animated.

Sharon was hovering outside his office door with her tablet computer in her hand. Vi and Jane Keene were back with heads bent over the screen on Vi's desk.

Jordan smiled at Sharon. "Have you got something for me, Constable?"

"Hope so, boss. I think I have anyway. Last night I went to talk to the girls again, like you said. I asked them specifically. They won't ever tell you nothing unless you ask and even then, they can be a bit tight-lipped. With everything that's happening, I'm worried about 'em."

Jordan raised his eyebrows and glanced at his watch.

"Sorry, sorry. So, I've found an address for the flats. What am I like? Why didn't I just ask them before? I'm kicking myself now. Good job you're on the ball, boss. Anyway, I reckon these might be them. It's some converted houses, big old ones in Wavertree. It was Suze that had all the info. Her and a mate were having a bit of a session and they were talking about Tilly, raising a glass and all that. Then this girl mentioned the flats. Well, we had to find her, the mate. Anyway, yeah, this girl had been friendly with Tilly for a bit. Actually, I don't think they were that friendly so much as Tilly had got her some gear now and then, way back when. Anyway, one thing led to another and they go on talking about these flats for ex-addicts."

"Detective, please. Can you cut to the chase? Did you get an address?"

"Yeah." Sharon held up her tablet screen towards him. "But there's more. When I got back, I traced the ownership through the Land Registry. So, to be clear, they're not owned by the clinic, which was something I had thought might be the case. So, that made me wonder if they were the right flats. I reckon they are, though. The odd thing is, they're owned by a charity, and it's not one I've heard of, and I couldn't get very far looking it up. That's dead weird, isn't it?"

"Yes, it is. But this is excellent work, Sharon. What we need to do now is get the forensic accountants on this and see what information there is about this charity and what the connection might be to the clinic or even the company that runs it."

"Yeah, I've already been in touch with them this morning and sent them what I had."

"Brilliant. Keep me informed and later we need to go to these flats and see if Tilly was there and if anyone remembers her. Later this morning."

"Me, boss?"

"Yes, you found the information."

"Ace, that's sound, great. I'm dead made up. I'll keep on at the forensic bods. Thanks, boss."

Jordan stood beside his desk in the incident room and it didn't take long for the hubbub to quieten. He was about to speak when the door opened, and Vickie Frost walked in.

"Morning everyone," she said. "I have news. Sorry, boss. Is it okay?"

Jordan nodded and smiled at her.

"Just come back from Allerton – posh house! My brilliant team have played a blinder. No surprise there, but you'll be pleased."

She spent the next ten minutes updating them on the search. The burglar alarm had been switched off and never re-set.

"That's something for you to get your head round, guys. Either it was never set, or the robber had the code, which is very sus. We have a couple of boxes of paperwork to go through. It was spread around a bit but it's what you would expect – invoices and so on. Some photographs. You're all dead impressed, are you not?"

There was a murmur from the others in the room and a couple of sarcastic claps.

"But I also have this." The sergeant leaned down and pulled a bag from the box she had carried in with her. She held up a small evidence bag. "Hidden in the kitchen in a tin full of flour. It was well wrapped, obviously, so not something you used on the spur of the moment and not something they wanted with them on their cruise."

"A phone," John said.

"See, that's why he's a detective!" This comment drew some laughter.

"It still held some charge and it isn't password-protected. I had a quick look and the call log hasn't been wiped. I imagine whoever it belongs to thought it was safe hidden away like that. Ha, that's got your attention, hasn't it? So, of course, I had a look. All suitable precautions were taken, before you start to get paranoid. Obviously, I was limited to what I could access – don't want to screw up any evidence. But what's our next step?" She paused. "Anybody, anybody?"

This drew a quiet laugh from some quarters and then Jordan put up his hand and said, "Our next step, miss, is to contact the provider for records."

Vickie winked and pointed at Jordan. "You win the lolly, Jordie, and a gold star. And finally, as if I haven't given you enough, I have the feed from the camera over the front door with a fairly decent image of someone who really does not look like a posh bloke who goes on cruises and is definitely not a posh bloke's wife. I've asked the techies to send you all a lovely little movie."

"That's brilliant, Vickie."

"But why are you surprised? Okay, got to go, work to do, but I've sent you a preliminary report with some images."

Vickie left and Jordan collected his jacket in preparation for the trip to Wavertree. The internal phone on his desk showed a call from Vi, and he glanced out of the doorway to see her waving at him.

"Sorry, boss. I know you're in a hurry, but when you have a minute, I need a word. Something I've been mulling over. I've already had a chat with DS Keene, and she agrees that it's something to consider. It's a bit 'out there', so I'd like to keep it just between us for the minute, if that's okay?"

"Soon as I get back."

Chapter 40

Jordan was aware of updates and messages pinging on his phone for the whole of the drive. Sharon offered to read them to him, but he didn't think he could cope with the inevitable chatter that would ensue. As it was, he could zone out and let the constant talking from the passenger seat become white noise. When they arrived outside the converted houses, there was a lot to read through.

The forwarded image from the security camera at the Griffiths' house was surprisingly clear. However, viewing it on his phone was nowhere near good enough and he wanted to zoom in on the partial shot they had of the intruder's face. There was enough to see that Vickie had been correct. The figure was slender and tall, obviously male, and dressed in tight jeans and a black jacket with some sort of logo. There was a note added at the end to say that Kath was already searching online for tops with the same design. There didn't seem to be a car parked nearby and when he left the house, he scurried away down the cul-de-sac.

Jordan asked Sharon to contact Stella and have a team out as soon as possible, looking for footage from any other security cameras on the properties nearby. If nothing came of this, he would need to justify his actions with the DCI, and up to now they had no concrete evidence that the Griffiths had been much more than witnesses. But if that were the case, why the disappearing act? No, he had to go with his gut.

Stella had sent a separate text to let him know that Mrs Vance and her sister-in-law were leaving Bath the next day and coming back to Liverpool. He made a note to take a printout of the spreadsheet when they went to see her. He could also let her know that an interim death certificate was available, which meant she could begin to arrange a funeral.

* * *

In Wavertree, two houses on the red-brick terrace had been knocked together. The front wall had been demolished to make a narrow parking space that could accommodate a small car. A porch had been fashioned in the alcove around the front door, and through the windows they could see umbrellas, a few pairs of trainers kicked off and pushed to one side, and a coat stand, with a couple of jackets slung on the hooks. There was just one bell push on the door frame.

They didn't have to wait long until a figure approached along the hallway and the light was switched on behind the frosted glass of the entrance. A tall man, probably late twenties, dressed in jeans and a grey jumper, swung the door open and stood with one hand on the handle, the other braced on the wall, frowning at them.

"We'd like a word, sir," Sharon said.

He leaned forward slightly to look at the warrant cards and then, with a sigh, stepped aside to let them in. Along the narrow hallway were two doors and a staircase to the upper floors. An archway beside the entrance connected to the second house. At the end of the corridor, the door to a kitchen stood open.

"Come in here," he said. "This is my room."

The bedsit was furnished with a narrow divan covered by a quilt. A couple of pillows squashed against the wall made a seat facing a large television on a wooden chest of drawers. There was a cupboard in the corner and bookshelves had been fitted into the chimney breast alcoves. It was clean and tidy, but the air was tainted with the smell of cigarette smoke. Next to the window, overlooking a scruffy back garden, was a small table and two chairs. The man waved a hand at this setup and sat on the edge of the bed.

"Right, I haven't got long. What is this about?"

"Do you want to tell us your name?" Jordan asked.

"Not really, but I suppose you'll insist. Gordon Warner. I'm the cleaner, manager, caretaker, whatever you want to call me. I keep the place straight and make sure the tenants don't get up to anything dodgy. They don't, so I don't know what you're doing here."

"How many tenants do you have?" Sharon asked as she took out her notebook and pen.

"Varies."

"Okay, how many flats are there?"

"Not really flats as such, more like rooms."

It was already obvious that this could be like pulling teeth. Jordan pursed his lips and looked slowly around the space. "Okay, mate. Cards on the table here. We're investigating a serious crime—"

"Nobody here has done nothing; believe me, they wouldn't."

"That remains to be seen, but if you're going to stay with this attitude, then things are going to be very sticky. I could insist you come down to the station. Trouble is, we're working out of St Anne Street. I can't take you in my car. It's not cleared for witness transport. We'll have to send for a squad car. Traffic at this hour of the day is diabolical and, on top of that, we have a shortage of staff. We could be looking at an hour, maybe more, when all we can do is sit and stare at each other. Then that'll take us to shift change by the time we get to the station. So, there'll be more delay." He paused and shook his head. "Or, you could just meet us halfway, answer our questions, fully and honestly, and this could be over before the tea goes cold."

"What tea?"

"Oh, I thought you said my colleague here could make us a cuppa."

"Alright. Come on. What's it all about?"

"Tea?" Jordan said.

"Oh, bloody hell, go on then. Use the bags in the box on the counter. Milk's in the fridge."

"Great," Jordan said.

Sharon went out into the corridor and they heard the water running followed by the click of the kettle switch. Jordan turned back to the manager.

"Right, we're trying to find out about a young woman who we believe lived here for a while and we'd like to know about her stay and when and why she left."

"Well, you can ask her, can't you? It's not a secret. People come and go. It's a sort of stopping off place. People coming out of the hostel for drug users stay for a bit and then move on. But you must know that, otherwise why come?"

"We can't ask her because, unfortunately, she's dead."

"Oh. Well, it's going to happen, isn't it?"

"What is?"

"People like these. I mean, when they come here, the hostel has sorted them out. When they leave, there's no knowing what's going to happen. They backslide, don't they? They're not here very long, most of 'em. I don't get too involved, just clean up and mind my own business."

"I wonder if you have come across the girl who was found in Ormskirk?"

"Don't know nothing about that."

"Her picture's been all over the place – in the newspapers, on the internet."

Gordon swept his arm in a wide arc. "See any computer?"

"No, but surely you have access to one, and as I say, she was in the paper."

"Alright, clever sod. I don't read, I don't have a computer, and I don't go online."

"I find that difficult to believe."

"Believe it." Gordon straightened his spine and looked Jordan in the eye. "I don't read, okay."

"But the books? They say otherwise." Jordan flicked a thumb towards the shelves.

Gordon stood, pulled out one of the paperbacks, and held it out for Jordan to see. It was a children's picture book. On the cover was a kitten and the title in bubble writing. He flipped open the front page to show more drawings of the cat with text in large font, simple words.

"That's what I read, okay? The other ones, those" – he pointed to paperback novels and a couple of hardbacks – "they've been left here by residents. I have 'em there so that one day, one day, I'll read them. For now, this is what I have. This is my homework from the free classes I take. So, now what do you have to say, mister policeman?"

Jordan was struggling to find words that wouldn't sound condescending. There were none available to him right then.

"I see."

"Yeah, you probably don't. Why do you think I'm stuck here in this shitty little room, cleaning up after a crowd of ex-druggies? We didn't all get the same deal. I'll bet you went to uni. What is it they call it, 'diversity'? Keeping the impression that it's fair for everyone. Well, it's not."

There was nowhere to take this conversation and no way Jordan was going to trade hard-luck stories about childhood with this man. He took out the printed image of Tilly that had been used in the paper.

"Do you recognise this girl?"

The outburst had cleared the air and Gordon was calmer now, not as antagonistic and defensive. "Is that her?"

"Yes."

"I've seen her around. Her name's Tammy, I think, or maybe Trixie, something like that. She knew some of the tenants. I think she'd been part of the scene, but I haven't seen her for a bit. She used to hang around a bit. Like I said, people backslide. I reckoned she'd just got back into the drug scene."

"So, she never lived here?"

"Not so far as I know; not while I've been here, anyway. I only got this job a few months ago."

Sharon entered the room carrying a tray of mugs. "Couldn't find no biscuits, boss," she said.

"Bloody hell, where do you think you are, the bloody Ritz?" Gordon said. "Look, I've got my cleaning to do, have this cuppa and then just bugger off. I've told you all I know. That Tammy, or whatever, isn't anything to do with me. She caused a fuss with the hostel one time, but I hadn't been here long enough to be involved in all of that. I haven't seen hide nor hair of her since. End of."

"Can you explain the fuss with the hostel?" Jordan said.

"Well, they told her to keep away. Said she was a bad influence on their residents. Matron comes regular, like. She tells me what to do and all of that."

"I'm not sure I understand you,"

"Aw Jesus. Like I said, this is a temporary place. They come here for a short time. Get the all-clear about their blood tests and all that, get fit, and then they move on – most of 'em. There's a couple stay longer. I'm not in the loop with all this. All I have to do is keep the place clean and make sure they go for their follow-up appointments and turn in the piss samples on time."

"It sounds as though you're more than a cleaner," Sharon said.

"Aye well, not really, but that's all dead easy. I wanted to be a nurse or one of them carers, but..." He wagged a hand toward the book that was lying on the shelf.

"Looks as though you're trying, though. You've got enough time to do that if you want to. What are you, twenty-five?" Jordan said.

"It's slow-going."

"But you've made a start."

"Maybe."

The atmosphere was friendlier now, and they drank the tea and chatted about the football and the weather. When they got up to leave, Jordan left his card with Gordon. The caretaker held out his hand and Jordan shook it.

"Thank you, Gordon. Good luck with your study."

"Ha, study. That's a posh word for it, but thanks."

As they climbed into their car, Gordon began to push the door closed only to have to open it again as a young man in jeans and an anorak turned into the path and went inside with a brief nod at the caretaker.

"So, what did you find?" Jordan asked as he pulled away from the kerb.

"I took some pictures," said Sharon. "Didn't get a chance to go upstairs with him leaving his door open. The kitchen was okay, clean, and the cupboards had all the packets and tins you'd expect. Decent stuff though, not all pound-shop Pot Noodles. The fridge and freezer were well stocked. One odd thing was a glass-fronted cupboard in the corner. It was locked, but from what I could see, it had all sorts of packets inside, like you see in the ozzy, you know. One of the drawers was full of little bottles, the sort the doctor gives you to pee in when you've got a UTI. I don't know if that's odd or not. Maybe, because they've been addicts, they have to sort of keep proving they're not taking anything to stay there."

"That makes sense. Pretty strict though, and I imagine they'd have to agree to it formally. Interesting."

Chapter 41

There was a lot going on and Jordan needed to sort it in his mind. So many threads – some of them would be vital, some would be tiny ticks that wouldn't count in the overall picture – but nothing could be missed. He needed time, but as soon as they arrived back in the incident room, there were calls for his attention.

John was about to visit his dad but wanted to talk to him about the phone from the Griffiths' house. Stella had stuff she needed to go through about Phoebe Vance, who was returning in the morning. Vi glanced up at Jordan as he passed her desk on his way to pour a cup of coffee. He nodded at her, acknowledging that he remembered she wanted to talk to him. He tapped his watch and held up five fingers.

First, he'd start with John, who already had his jacket on and a plastic bag of treats for the patient in his hand.

"I've sent a note through, but you need to look at it soon as. The phone we found at the Griffiths' had just a very few numbers on it. We're trying to trace them. Obviously, we've tried ringing them, but no luck. So far, we've just been able to identify one of the regular contacts – Rose Heath, the matron from the clinic. A few are international. When the provider gets back to us, we'll know more about those."

Jordan nodded and pursed his lips. "That is interesting. Mind you, he's a businessman, so international calls are not that unusual, but why on a hidden phone? Dodgy business dealings could explain why they cut and run, I suppose. But why the matron?"

"We didn't ring her. Don't want to give her the heads-up."

Jordan agreed it all needed looking at more closely, and he would get to it as soon as possible.

He took his coffee into the little-used office. Perhaps he should close the door, just give himself space, but there was no time for that, and it went against everything he tried to do, encouraging everyone to work as a team.

He used the internal phone to speak to Stella. "What's happening?"

"I've made an appointment for us to see Mrs Vance tomorrow afternoon. I spoke to the cleaner to find out what time she was due back. She was a bit leery, boss."

"Well, she doesn't exactly like us, does she?"

"No, I know, but it was something else. Anyway, long story short, she asked us to get there early to have a chat. She's in tomorrow to do a final clean before the 'lady of the house' comes back and to receive the Waitrose order, because heaven forbid that the woman has to unpack her own eggs. Oh yeah, and when you have time, Vi wants a word, but it's something her and Jane Keene have been talking about. By the way, Jane asked if you could give her an update on today. I think she feels a bit left out, and she needs to report to her boss. Not that there's been much for her to do, really."

Jordan looked at his watch. It was nearly end of shift, but there was still a backlog of work. He blew out his cheeks. "Okay, just give me a minute."

Chapter 42

Jordan looked at the report on the calls from the Griffiths' hidden phone. The timings of the contact with the matron were interesting. Mostly they were evenings, very early mornings, or weekends. So, not during working hours. Was this all about an affair?

Jordan stared at the list and something just out of reach tickled at the back of his memory. He began to go through the records again, hoping whatever it was would become clear.

His phone rang. There was no name on the screen. The voice on the other end of the line was male and vaguely familiar. The caller double-checked who he was talking to before he introduced himself.

"It's Jez, from the squat."

Jordan swung his chair away from the desk and frowned. "Jez, good to hear from you."

"You probably won't think so. I'm just ringing to let you know Bren's gone."

"How do you mean?"

"Well, simple, not here. Gone. I went down the town to see if I could get some scran from the food bank and when I got back, she'd just buggered off. She's not well, but she'd taken all her stuff, so I reckon that's it, for now at least. I hope she's okay, but between you and me, I doubt it."

"You had no idea that she was thinking about leaving?"

"Nope. I thought she was too knackered, to be honest. You saw her, saw the state she was in. Anyway, just thought I'd let you know."

"If she comes back, will you give me a ring?"

"Not happening, mate, sorry. I'm moving on. The landlord wants to bring the cleaners in now and get the place ready for new tenants."

"Where will you go?"

"Not a clue. Just somewhere. Don't expect I'll see her again, but if I do, I'll let her know you want a word. How about that?"

"Brilliant, thanks. Take care, Jez."

Jordan let the team know about the new development. Stella said that, although she was sorry and worried about the girl, she wasn't sure how much it would hamper their enquiries and there was a mutter of agreement. Sharon agreed to talk to Suze and ask about any contact she'd had with Brenda. Vi offered to stay late to go through the town centre cameras that they had access to in the hope that they would pick up sightings of her. Jordan promised he'd try to get her overtime. They all knew that with no idea which direction Bren had gone, nor the exact time she had left, it was a forlorn hope. They had to try, not least because the girl was vulnerable and there had already been two murders.

"I checked on that big bloke from the hostel, by the way," Sharon said. "Not exactly a nice man. Been questioned a couple of times about fights and what have you, but nothing ever stuck. He did work for a while as a bouncer, but that was up in Scotland. Funny change of profession, but that's all I could find."

It had been a frustrating day and then the internal phone rang, inviting Jordan up to the DCI's office to join the gold team and deliver a status update. He buried his head in his hands and groaned.

Chapter 43

He drew the curtains even though it wasn't quite dark. It was better to watch his videos and for practising. He changed into the kit and went through his preparations. The furniture was all against the walls. There had to be space. Then, he turned on the mood lights. This, for him, was holy. Not like when he was a kid, and they'd been dragged to St Jude's twice every Sunday and he'd been forced to be an altar boy. That was just stupid old people, brainwashed and pathetic. No, this was holy and real and meant something. This led somewhere. This would make him famous.

Back then, when he'd been small, his gran had told him he should find pleasure in the world around him. She was like that, his gran. She was always coming out with stuff that sounded stupid, as if she'd read it on a meme. But they didn't have them in those days. Not as far as he knew. How could they? She was an antwacky old woman. Well, not anymore. She was long dead.

He'd liked his gran really, though, in spite of the religion. She made great roast dinners for afterwards. Not like his mam and her horrible beans and chips. Anyway, she'd been right. That girl in the squat was part of the world around him. Part of the world he was building for himself, anyway. He had taken real pleasure in that.

He could still remember her face when he showed her the pictures of that bitch in Ormskirk. It had been a rush. Deffo worth taking them while he'd been there. Yes, it had been a risk while she was still warm, still bleeding. But he'd been careful. He'd turned off the auto upload thing, and he hadn't sent them to anyone. God, that look on her face, and then she started snivelling. It made him feel so good, watching her fall to bits.

When he saw that druggie down in the city, he'd known what he should do. He'd been right, he'd scared her good and proper, turned her into a snivelling blob, spaced out in a corner. He could have finished her off there and then but that bloke had turned up, gegging in, taking her away. He could kill him, slice him up, and leave him in the gutter.

Maybe he should do the same thing again, this time with that other woman. Snotty bitch, her and her tame thug. Wonder if she'd fall apart like that when she saw that doctor, bleeding all over the floor. It was a shame he couldn't share them. Maybe one day. When he was famous and everyone was talking about him. When he was as famous as all those American killers. Yeah, he could do it then. Maybe he could put them on the dark web, though. Best not. The bizzies were probably on there. They're stupid, but it was a risk. Better not, not yet.

It was time to move on, though. That girl knew too much now. He could off her if he wanted. She'd run away, though, and he'd have to go looking. He should have thought of that and taken care of her straight away. Cameras everywhere. He was careful, but it was always a risk. No, she wasn't worth it. She wasn't special, just a druggy, probably a prozzy as well. He reckoned she'd be too scared to talk. More than likely she'd be trying to hide, trying to get away, had to be. There was no way she was going to last long, state she was in. Anybody could see that and then he could forget about her. She wouldn't be a problem anymore. But he needed more money so he could bail, now, soon as.

Soon he would leave this manky room and get himself something nicer. Maybe he could go to Southport, over to the Wirral, he could go anywhere if he wanted. Get himself sorted and then look for another job. But before that, there was something important he needed to do.

Chapter 44

By the time Jordan joined the gold team in DCI Trent's office, everyone was watching the clock. Their impatience to leave worked in his favour as Jordan delivered a brief rundown of progress. He gave it some spin, concentrating on the positives, steering away from the dead ends and frustrations, and hoping no-one would start talking about the time passing and the trail going cold. He caught a look from the DCI which let him know he was fully aware of the positive tone he was putting on it, but a nod and the hint of a smile also said that he understood, and they weren't in trouble. Yet.

He went back to the incident room to collect his jacket. The team had left and there was a note from Stella to tell him they were meeting in the pub for a quick bevvy before they headed off.

He was tired and wasn't sure he wanted to bother, but then he thought about Vi and her constant attempts to speak to him and these casual meetings away from the office were often very useful. He called Penny to let her know he'd be late.

It was ten minutes on foot to the pub. He'd heard of it, named after Liverpool's reputedly most famous landlady, but not had the chance to visit. He wished this occasion was under better circumstances but the walk gave him time to unwind and when he arrived at Ma Egerton's, Jordan was glad that he'd decided to join the team. The place was busy with end-of-day office workers, the usual smattering of tourists and theatregoers enjoying early evening food and drink. The atmosphere was happy and relaxed.

Kath and Vi were sharing a huge pizza with Stella, and Jordan was surprised to see John with a bowl of scouse and a Guinness.

"Your dad okay?" Jordan asked.

"He's asleep and then it's their teatime, so I thought I'd come here and have some scran and catch up. What can I get you, boss?"

"No, my shout."

Jordan took the drink orders and when he came back with the tray of glasses, he pulled a chair up to the corner where Kath and Vi were deep in conversation.

He waited until the chat moved on and then leaned close to Vi. "I'm sorry. I know you wanted a word," he said.

"Oh, yes. It's just an idea. To be honest, the more I've thought about it, the dafter it sounds. I was going to let it go, but then Jane Keene said, no, I should mention it."

"Okay, I'm listening."

The DC took a deep breath. There followed a meandering explanation about her daughter's boyfriend, who she didn't really like because he was 'weird and away with the fairies half the time.' Jordan gave her the space. She had earned it with her patience. She told him that she had arrived home one evening to find her daughter in the living room with the boyfriend.

"He was wearing a black jacket and then these really dodgy pant things. Anyway, he had this big stick, and he was waving it around and dancing about. Turns out it was some sort of martial art. Now, that made me think of that thing on the tele years ago with the bloke who was a monk. I had to look it up to remind myself, but it was called *Kung Fu*. Do you remember it?"

Jordan shook his head.

"Sorry, boss. What I'm saying is that watching the bloke my girl's with and then looking at the film on the tele, it's a ritual, isn't it? It wasn't kung fu, something else. Oh, I know, kendo, that was it."

Jordan shook his head again. "Sorry I'm still not really with you."

"Well, they practise the same moves over and over. With the stick thing, so why not a sword or a big knife? Then the same moves would mean the same wounds. Like I say, it's probably me being dead stupid."

Before Jordan had time to respond, Kath, who had listened to the conversation, passed her phone along the table. "Bloody hell, boss. Look?"

The image was of a hoody with a logo on it – a red disc with a dark figure in silhouette.

"I've been looking all over and soddin' Google sends me that as an advert cos I searched 'martial arts'."

Chapter 45

John was out early the following morning touring the many martial arts clubs. It was a frustrating exercise because most of them were closed and the people he was able to speak to, mainly cleaners and caretakers, merely glanced at the image he showed them and suggested he come back later when they were open for training.

It was tedious and dispiriting, but Stella and Sharon said they would take over while John went to see his dad.

Back in the incident room, Kath was staring at the screen, noting every movement around the squat on the afternoon that Brenda had disappeared. They knew she had been there when Jez had left. He was away for a few hours, sitting outside a shop in the town centre with an empty paper cup in the hope of getting a bit of cash, and then at the food bank where he met a friend with whom he spent a while drinking a couple of cans of lager and watching the ships at the Pier Head.

Jordan walked to the Vances' house in Canning Street where he turned up just as the Waitrose van arrived with the grocery delivery. Gilly piled carrier bags onto the worktop and pulled open the huge fridge. Jordan stood quietly in the kitchen until she had put away the perishables, but when she then began to unpack packets of biscuits and bags of flour, he interrupted.

"You're having a laugh? Come on, Gilly, you said you wanted to talk to me before Mrs Vance came back."

"Oh, she'll be ages yet," said Gilly. "She rang to say she was going to stop for lunch on the way."

"You couldn't let me know?"

She grinned at him. "Okay." She offered him coffee, and he thought the chat might go better if they sat together with a drink.

Once she'd served the mugs, she sat across the table from him and took a gulp of the coffee. "Right, I'm not a gossip. I'm not. I keep my neb out of other people's business. But I was a bit freaked, to be honest, and decided to let you know."

Jordan waited.

"I came down yesterday. It was a bit late because my old fella had wanted me to go down the pub with him for a swift half, but I wanted to get a start on things before today. Normally, I'm gone from here long before evening, but with nobody here, I thought it'd be okay."

She stopped and glanced at the window, which overlooked the back garden.

"It was out there. They've got them lights, the ones that come on when you walk in front of them. Anyway, nearly scared me outta my skin when the damn things clicked on. It was drizzling rain and just dark enough for them to be working. So, I had the lights on in the rooms and it was hard to see. But I thought I saw something and, well, I had. There was a bloke outside, in the garden, standing by that pergola thing. I went closer to the window, and he stepped nearer to the house. Must have seen me moving. Well, I was bricking it by then and I go to get my phone out and he bends forward and like peers in. He lifted his hand up and gave a sort of wave. I held my phone up to let him know I was going to dial. He turned round and legged it across the grass. He jumped up on that wall and he was gone."

"Do you have any idea who it might have been?"

"'course I bloody don't. It was nearly dark, and I was scared shitless."

"How tall was he?"

"Nearly as tall as you, but skinny. Not that you're fat or nothing, but he was dead thin. Ran quick, so I'd say he was youngish but not a kid."

"Could you tell what he was wearing?"

"Not really. Dark clothes, I would say a hoody. I'm just going by the shape, you know; you couldn't see his neck properly."

"We'll need a statement. It could be important. Will you come to St Anne Street?"

"I suppose so. Once herself is back and paid me. It's not the first time."

"How do you mean?"

"Not the first time I've seen young blokes in the garden. Times she was away, while himself was still alive. Coupla times, I never said nothing, but I reckon they was here to see him. You know, see him, see him."

Jordan shook his head. "Sorry, I'm not sure I know what you mean."

"Oh, for Christ's sake. What I'm saying is that the door swung both ways with him. With Mr Vance. When she was away, he'd play, but you know…" She gave a wriggle of her shoulders, which meant nothing, but Jordan suddenly understood.

"Are you saying Roland Vance was bisexual?" Jordan said.

"Duh." Gilly gave a laugh. "Doesn't bother me what he does, only the sneaking about's a bit much and the one in the garden mustn't have known about him being dead. But, when you think about it, that's really odd because it's been on the telly and in the paper and everything. There were even flowers left by the gate a coupla times." She paused briefly and pursed her lips. "I didn't know whether to tell you or not. I've gone back and forth in my mind but I talked to my old fella and he said to let you know. Said it could be important and if I didn't, I could be in trouble."

Jordan arranged for the cleaner to call into the station on her way home and make a statement. He felt obliged to tell her to take care. She nodded and smiled at him.

"Thanks. I'm not daft but, thanks."

There was no point hanging around waiting for the widow to arrive so Jordan walked back to the police station, trying to find a connection between this new information, the new evidence, and everything they already knew.

Kath rang as he turned into the building. He told her he'd be with her in moments, but she couldn't wait to let him know that she'd found footage of a man outside the squat who had knocked on the door and spoken briefly to someone. Within the next half an hour, Brenda was seen leaving, barely able to stand but leaning on the wall as she hurried away.

"I think it's one of the blokes from Ormskirk, boss. I'm nearly sure. A copy has already gone to Jane Keene. I'm waiting for her to get back to me. Not only that–"

She turned and clicked off her mobile as Jordan burst into the room and rushed across to her desk. She turned the screen so that he had a better view of the montage of images.

"Look. It's the same bloke. It's all the same bloke. He's one of the blokes travelling alone on the train to Ormskirk, it's him at the Griffiths' and the squat. Boss, it's him. Look at the way he stands, the way he hunches his shoulders. He leans a bit to one side. Look at his skinny legs and tight jeans." She pointed at the monitor. "We are looking at him, aren't we?"

"Can you print out a copy and ask Sharon to take it to the Vances' before Gilly leaves? Soon, before Mrs Vance comes home. See if she thinks it could be the intruder. Brilliant work, Kath."

Chapter 46

While he was skimming through overnight reports, a chime on his computer alerted Jordan to a message from Vi. He flipped to his email to find a report on the Griffiths. They were both Liverpool born and bred. Frederick Griffith had gone to The Blue Coat School and then to the LSE where he had graduated with a degree in economics. They had met while Pauline was working in London for a fashion house, but it wasn't clear just what her role had been. Her schooling had been less exclusive, and she had dropped out of a design course at Lancaster University without graduating. They had been married for twenty-seven years.

The report began to get more interesting at this point. Frederick had left the firm he was working for and set up an import business. For a while they brought in all sorts of things, including fashion items. As time went by, they began to specialise in uniforms for cleaners and nurses. Then later the firm became focussed on hospital supplies, dressings and instruments.

According to Vi, the Griffiths were providing medical supplies to the clinic; in fact, to the whole group of clinics. She made mention of a website where the goods were being sold, but she had not had any reply to her enquiries as to the whereabouts of Mr and Mrs Griffiths or their last contact.

Obviously, without a warrant, they would be unable to look at their accounts, and although there was an all-ports alert out, there was still no hint of where they may have gone. Vi mentioned that the import business dealt with goods coming from China and Jordan hoped the couple hadn't been missed flying out.

He typed a thank-you response and set off to see Mrs Vance. Walking back and forth around the city was a definite benefit to being based in the main headquarters, and he knew he would miss it when they were reassigned to Copy Lane, where most places involved a drive and there wasn't the city centre vibe which he knew was special. He had once turned down the option to work here permanently and was still convinced he'd done the right thing despite the city buzz and the exercise.

While she had been away, Phoebe Vance appeared to have recovered somewhat. Her hair was neatly styled and she was dressed in soft wool pants and a silk blouse. The dark rings that had been under her eyes were less visible and she had carefully applied make-up.

She didn't offer coffee and when she sat, it was on the edge of the settee in the living room. Jordan was aware of the sister-in-law passing the door with bags and carrying them upstairs.

"I won't keep you long," he said.

The response was a slight incline of her head.

"I would like you to have a look at this image. I'm afraid it's not terribly clear, but I wonder if you recognise this person."

Phoebe took the printout and held it up to the light from the window. She studied it for a couple of moments. "Who is this?"

"At the moment, we haven't been able to identify him, but we think he is probably involved in the recent crimes."

"Well, I don't know who he is. I've never seen him. It's a very poor photograph, anyway."

"You have no idea who this might be?"

"No. I don't, and really why would I?"

"We hoped you might, especially as your cleaner was shown this earlier and is very much under the impression that it's someone who she saw in your garden recently."

Phoebe Vance raised a hand to her throat and Jordan noticed the widening of her eyes, but when she spoke, she sounded calm.

"Well, Gilly can be excitable. I should think it's best to take anything she says with a pinch of salt. We have security lights and alarms. Why would anyone be in the garden? I'm sorry, Mr Carr, I can't help you and I'm very busy. Thank you for letting me know about the death certificate. I now have a funeral to arrange, and my husband was a popular and well-loved man. His funeral must reflect our standing in the community. I owe it to him, so there is a lot of work to be done. If you could see yourself out, I'd be grateful."

She had put on a good show but hadn't been able to still the slight quiver in her fingers and the sudden pulse visible in her throat. Jordan wondered if her unwillingness to show him to the door was more inability to stand steadily rather than rudeness.

* * *

When Jordan arrived back at St Anne Street, Stella and Sharon were drinking coffee and eating doughnuts. They looked tired and unhappy. They'd had no luck at any of the martial arts clubs in the city. The problem was partly the poor-quality image. Vi had done her best. The footage that they had was already with the technical department, and a bloke who was generally referred to as 'the geek' had agreed to stay after his shift to work on what they had.

"He wasn't that impressed, boss," Vi said. "Not only are the images blurry from movement, but none of them have a direct view of his face, not straight on."

She looked exhausted, her eyes were bloodshot, and he told her to go home. She didn't argue. Stella and Sharon called in to say they were done for the day and a phone conversation with John at the hospital was worrying as his father had deteriorated over the last couple of days.

"I thought we were going to have more time, boss. Now, it just seems as though he's given up." The DC was too upset to talk for long.

Chapter 47

As the sky darkened and street lights outside came on, the sounds around the station changed. The workplace chatter was replaced by the hum of vacuum cleaners and slamming doors from the car park as the day staff left for home. Jordan opened his laptop. He couldn't shake the feeling that he was missing something. A detail was there, but he couldn't grasp it. He looked at the images of the victims, the missing Griffith couple, the new information about the figure in the garden and the startling declaration that Mr Vance was gay or bisexual. Did his wife know? There was no doubt it was something Jordan would have to address with her. He had only put it off because of her comments about the cleaner being unreliable. It was the wrong time and could have invited denial or outrage, which would have got him nowhere. There had to be more evidence. He contacted Sharon.

The PC had already put in a long day, but she was keen and willing to head out into the night-time gay scene to ask around the regulars at the bars and clubs and on the streets.

"Take one of the uniforms with you," Jordan said.

Sharon named one of the junior constables who had been seconded to the team. "I know her from school. Well, she was a coupla years below me, but she knew my sister. She'll be ace. She's gay, so she'll know the best places to go."

Jordan planned to interview the clinic staff the next day, as discretely as possible. There were so many possibilities to consider. And yet, that wasn't the niggle in his mind, though. It was something that he just couldn't bring into focus.

He poured himself more coffee but drank a tumbler of water to offset the caffeine, and then opened the spreadsheet John had been working on and stared at the rows of initials and dates. This had to be significant. He needed to make sure they were chasing the airlines for manifests. There was no reason for these records to be hidden if it was simply a calendar of meetings or maybe a note of shipping orders? Why was the phone hidden? As the thoughts unwound in his tired brain, the link connected. He opened a split screen and compared the calls from the phone found in the tin in the house in Allerton and the times on the spreadsheet, and it was all there in front of him. Someone had called the matron within a couple of hours of the flights leaving John Lennon Airport. Flights heading for various destinations in Europe. He leaned closer and peered at the screen.

It really was time to make an appointment at the opticians.

There were clearly calls on the days of the flights but then others a few days later, which did not coincide with outward flights. They could conceivably be seen as random, but every flight was covered. He tried to clear his mind, to let the thoughts develop without forcing them.

The calls were brief. A couple of minutes for each one. That didn't seem like a chat between lovers, which had been a possibility that had crossed his mind. Surely, the matron wasn't taking holidays that often, and the evidence hadn't suggested that she was employed by the import business.

Rose Heath was connected to the clinic, the inpatient facility and, it seemed, the halfway house for recovered addicts.

Frederick Griffith was connected to the clinic via his import trade. His wife was a patient there and a witness to the death of Mr Vance. He had assumed that Frederick

Griffith and Roland Vance were the type to belong to the Masons. Indeed, the chief constable's interest backed that up. He hadn't needed Ted Bliss to point that out. But the web was tangled. He crossed to the whiteboard and drew lines from one to the other and to the image of the spreadsheet. It didn't help much, but surely, the main connection had to be the matron.

He sent a message to Stella for her to meet him at the clinic early the next morning. The senior nurse had been away when the murder had happened, but that didn't mean she hadn't been involved. But then, what could she have to do with the death of poor Tilly in Ormskirk? By now, his mind was in turmoil and his shoulders and neck ached from leaning over the desk. He'd worked out what had been niggling at him, but it had only thrown up more questions.

It was time to take a break, to pack up and go home to see Penny and let his mind unwind. They needed the first domino to fall and that would bring the whole thing down. It would come, it always did, but it had to come soon.

Chapter 48

A couple of girls heading home from a party in the early hours found Brenda curled unconscious in a shop doorway. They might have staggered past if her belongings hadn't been strewn across the pavement. She was taken to the Royal Hospital in an ambulance. The account was on the overnight reports that Jordan scanned while he was waiting for his coffee to brew. The A&E department eventually confirmed she was there, unconscious, and still in a cubicle waiting to be admitted.

He called Sharon on the hands-free as he drove to work. Though Bren was not fit to be interviewed, he told PC Taylor to go straight to the hospital.

"They wouldn't tell me anything much on the phone. We need to know if she has been attacked or has taken drugs, maybe too many, accidentally, deliberately, all of that. The minute they'll let you have access, get her to look at the picture. See if she can put a name to the bloke who caused her to run. If you can get a name, or there's any major change, call me immediately."

"On it, boss. I've sent you an email, by the way. I was going to give you a buzz last night, but it was dead late, and I thought I might wake your little boy. You wouldn't have appreciated that. Only I know you worked late, and you must be bloody exhausted."

"Was there anything specific?"

"Sorry, I'm rabbiting again, aren't I?"

"A bit, yes."

"Okay, sorry, I'll try to put it in a nutshell. That Vance bloke was deffo into men. No doubt. I talked to a lad last night who knew him. I went down Stanley Street in the gay district. Some of the regulars down there know me from hanging around with Suze. There was a few of them around and one guy approached me after they told him who I was. He was gutted, to be honest. Seems as though he really liked Roland Vance. Apart from anything else, he was generous with gifts and money and was kind, like. He had specific preferences, but nothing dodgy. There was no talk of anything other than him just liking young men, preferred them slim and fit, apparently. He met them at his house sometimes, or now and again he'd book hotel rooms. Nothing in the Pool, over on the Wirral or out round St Helens, Southport and like that. He was in the closet for certain. Paid for taxis but wouldn't have them in his car and always made them come round the back of the house. Never saw them at the clinic. Chas was pretty clear about that. There was a bit of sneaking around, but the ones that knew him felt sorry for him more than anything. He was loaded, but not happy. Anyway, this Chas had a few sessions with him, if you know what I mean, but he rated him. Called him a gentleman. He's been off in Cyprus and hadn't heard about the murder until just yesterday. I'll keep on asking around if you like."

"So, there's no chance of this Chas being the figure in the garden, then?"

"No, he showed me his plane tickets on his phone and loads of pictures from his trip. I tried to find out if there were other regulars, but it seems as though Vance didn't do that. He'd have a couple of meets and then on to the next. I wondered if he thought that was protecting himself, you know, not getting too deep in with any one bloke. It wasn't about relationships, just the physical stuff and some company, I reckon."

"Will Chas give us a statement?" Jordan said.

"Ah, now that's a different matter. I don't think so – bad for business and that sort of thing gets around. He was happy enough to speak off the record, mainly because he was upset and actually a bit scared. You know, it was all a bit close to home, and he'd heard about Tilly. They all know about her, 'course they do, and they're freaked out."

"Okay. Leave that with me."

He parked his car and left immediately for the walk to Canning Street and another chat with Phoebe Vance. Things were beginning to move but not in a direction he had anticipated. On the way to visit the widow, he passed by the clinic to pick up Stella and share the new information.

Carol answered the door and didn't bother to hide the sigh and the roll of her eyes. "I hope you've come to report some sort of progress," she said.

"We have a couple of questions for your sister-in-law and it might be helpful if we can have a chat with you, when it's convenient," Jordan told her.

"I suppose if you must, but I don't know what you think I can tell you. I loved my brother, I miss him. We were close when we were children and he was my nearest living relative. I am lost without him," Carol said.

He anticipated that this would be a tricky interview. If Phoebe didn't know about her husband's secret life, he might be about to shatter all that she knew about the man she was married to. He was prepared for tears and shock and probably denial. What he wasn't prepared for was the level of anger she expressed when she demanded that he leave the house immediately and that she would not speak to him again.

"If the police need any more information from me, then I will speak to your superiors. How dare you come to my home where we are grieving and spout filthy lies?"

He would have pointed out that if there were lies being told, they were not his. He wanted her to understand how significant this could be in the search for her husband's killer. But there was no way to make her listen.

She stood and ushered him out of the room, stomped along the hallway and tossed her head as she opened the door. "Get out, and if anyone from the police wants to speak to me or my sister-in-law again, it cannot be you and they will need to make an appointment."

They had no option but to leave and as the door slammed behind them, Stella turned in time to see the sister-in-law watching from behind the drapes.

Chapter 49

"Blimey, boss, she was a bit miffed," Stella said.

"I expected a reaction," Jordan said, "but I thought maybe she already knew and so there would be – oh, I don't know – embarrassment, maybe a sort of acceptance and perhaps relief that she no longer had to carry the secret, if that's what it was. If she didn't know there would be shock, of course, but she went for out-and-out fury."

"That's a funny way to put it."

"It might just be the way I was reading it, but it was so quick. She went from nothing to anger. Wouldn't you have thought she'd have been surprised or disbelieving first? Why was she so furious with us?"

"Not sure I see where you're going with this, boss."

"Okay, to put it bluntly, my feeling was that she already knew. She wasn't upset by the information, she was angry because we knew about it and wanted to address it. Did you see the sister-in-law's face?"

"I saw her watching us when we left. She was hiding."

"Yes, but there was no shock at all either. She didn't seem upset until Phoebe Vance began to rant and that was more of a reaction to the row than anything else."

"Yeah, now you mention it. I don't think she said anything, did she?"

"You've got a brother, haven't you?" he asked.

"Yeah, pain in the arse, him and his girlfriend. The little kid's okay, but he's so spoiled. Sorry, irrelevant. I'm doing a Sharon."

"What?"

"It's what people say when anyone goes off on a tangent. God, she can talk."

Jordan laughed. "It's annoying at times and she really needs to get it under control. See what's happened now, we've started meandering ourselves."

"Sorry, you were talking about the sister."

"Yep. So, if your brother were gay, you'd know, right?"

"Too bloody true, 'course I'd know. You talk about that stuff, don't you?"

"Yes, and she has told us they were close as they were growing up. I think it's safe to assume that she would have known if he was an in-the-closet gay or maybe bi. If it were your brother, wouldn't you say something to his future wife?"

"Oh, I don't know, boss. Sometimes those relationships, the ones with in-laws, they're hard, aren't they?"

"But they're close. Who did Phoebe Vance call to come to help her when he was killed? She didn't ask for a friend or anyone nearby, she went straight to the sister-in-law who had to come back from abroad."

"Yeah, that's true."

"What now?"

"Now we are going to have a word with the matron, so back to the clinic. Give Sharon a call, see what's going on with Brenda."

Stella made the call and shook her head. "She's still out for the count. There are no injuries, though. Nothing that looks as though she was attacked. The doctor thinks it was an overdose and they're treating her for that, but she's not a well person anyway, apparently. They reckon she's had some sort of surgery recently. They're doing a scan as soon as they can to find out just what's going on."

"What sort of surgery?"

"Abdominal, but they don't want to say more than that right now."

"Hmm. I guess we could ask the matron about that. We know the girl had been in the recovery hostel, so they must have had her medical records. In any case, I think that's something we need to find out about. So, the matron and then on to the hospital. We need to drive. Is your toy car charged up?"

"Cheeky bugger. Yes, it is."

Chapter 50

The clinic was clean and newly decorated. The smell of coffee and flowers filled the reception area and staff in uniform bustled back and forth. No patients were around, but the receptionist told them they were slowly working towards resuming their usual services and Mr Vance's clients were now being treated by other consultants from within the group. The matron was in her office at the rear of the ground floor.

Rose Heath had lost some of the holiday tan and the lines around her eyes seemed to have deepened during the few days since they had last seen her. Possibly because of the stress of trying to manage the clinic with the medical director gone and, of course, the sadness of losing a close colleague. Additionally, there must be pressure from head office. It was likely that the recent events had lost them clients. Vivienne Campbell, the manager, appeared to be weathering the storm better. She smiled at them as they walked along the corridor, offered them coffee and ordered one of the nursing assistants to organise it when they accepted.

In the matron's office, the welcome was cool, and though they were asked to sit, the woman didn't meet their gaze but shuffled papers on her desk and swivelled her chair to look at the computer screen.

"We might not need to keep you long," Jordan told her. "I can see you're very busy. We have some queries about calls to your mobile phone. We need to clarify just what they were regarding."

As he spoke, he saw her throat work, and she stopped fiddling with the mouse and turned to look at them. "My phone? What on earth has my phone to do with anything?"

Stella took out her notebook and made much of flipping through the pages. "The patient, Pauline Griffith, who found Mr Vance…" she said. She waited as the matron struggled not to react.

"Yes?"

"She is missing, along with her husband."

"Is she? Well, I don't understand. What has that got to do with me?"

Jordan took the printout from the file he was carrying. On it was the list of calls from the phone found in the flour tin at the Griffiths' house. Many of them were highlighted in yellow. The others had been redacted.

"These are calls to you from a phone found at their home. The fingerprints on the phone confirm it has been handled by Frederick Griffith. There are quite a number of calls over a protracted period. The couple are persons of interest in the inquiry into Mr Vance's murder. So…" He waited.

There was a sharp knock on the door and the assistant brought in a tray of coffee and biscuits. While the palaver of serving the drinks went on, the matron turned away from the desk and reached for a box of tissues on a bookcase behind her. As she pulled out the thin paper handkerchief, her fingers shook. She blinked hard, but not quickly enough to hide the glint of moisture in her eyes as she blew her nose and cleared her throat.

She straightened her spine and placed her hands on the desk with the fingers clasped together. "I'm not sure what you're asking me, Detective Inspector."

"I thought I'd made it clear. We would like you to explain what the calls were about."

"And if I refuse?"

"Then I will obtain a warrant which will give me permission to examine the data, to search your office here and your home. It may take some time and while we wait,

I'll ask you to come with us back to the station so that we can have a longer chat about just what the connection is between you and the Griffith couple."

Rose Heath was struggling. She tried to convince them it was all to do with Pauline Griffith's treatment. When Jordan asked if it was usual for patients to have her personal number, there was a garbled comment about the Griffiths being friends of the clinic. Jordan pointed out that there was a clinic manager and the main clinic number, neither of which showed calls from the couple. The matron simply shrugged her shoulders and gazed at the top of her desk.

"I think this would be a lot easier if you were more straightforward with us," Stella said. "The more you try to wriggle around this, the worse it is. We are already assuming you have something to hide. This is a murder inquiry. As it stands, we could make a case that you are obstructing the police. You really don't want to go down this road. Come on, Rose, why were they calling you so often and do you know where they are now?"

Chapter 51

It might really be time to go. The bizzies were sniffing around. He'd seen them again, back at that woman's house. The big black bloke and one of his birds.

He walked along the riverfront and for a moment he stopped to look at the Beatles statues in front of the Liver Building. Jammy sods. They had it made. Played a couple of tunes, ponced about with their floppy hair and they were minted in no time.

It was drizzling rain. The lights shone out, pooling on the shiny flagstones as the river slid past dark and moody. A ferry was crossing, and he watched gulls wheeling above the wake, luminous against dark clouds. He loved this place. It was rough in parts, and sometimes violent, but then, so was he. He was a son of the city, a Scouser, and now he was going to have to go. He should never had got involved. He'd needed money though, and this had got him some but it wasn't enough. He saw that now. He should have asked for more up front. Now he'd do it, he'd say he needed extra because he was going to have to leave.

He hadn't been paid for going to the posh house in Allerton either. It hadn't been his fault he didn't find the phone. There was no sodding phone, same as there was no sodding money. They'd used him, all of them, they'd used him. Well, now he'd show them.

He went back to his room. It wasn't even a decent place to live, not really, not worth the cost of having to leave. He packed his bag. There wasn't much, but he took the posters and the bamboo stick and asked the bloke downstairs to look after them for a bit. He wasn't keen but then changed his mind when he was bunged a couple of quid.

At the house, he stowed his bag behind a purple bin left out for collection and shinned over the garden wall. The light was on in the kitchen and another in an upstairs room. This wouldn't take long, *and then he'd sort the other stuff. He tapped on the kitchen door and waited.*

Chapter 52

When his phone rang, Jordan left Stella with the matron and stepped into the corridor. Kath Webster told him the Griffiths had been spotted by a border control officer who was reviewing CCTV for something else entirely. They were disembarking from the ferry in Holyhead.

"We've had a look now, and they were on the boat from Jersey to Dublin and then over to Wales. They obviously made a run from Gran Canaria before the BOLO notice had gone out. Jammy sods. She's either got a wig or changed her hair colour, but that's all. It's a long and roundabout route from where they left the cruise ship. Thing is, though, they could do a lot of that without showing their passports, just approved photo ID for travel from Jersey. He obviously knows about the Common Travel Area. They really are dodgy, aren't they, boss?"

"I don't think there's any doubt about that, but just how dodgy remains to be seen," Jordan said.

"Whatever they did, nothing alerted the border patrol guys until this one guy who was on the ball."

She had already put out an alert, letting everyone know the couple were now on UK soil.

"I'll get on to the DCI and organise an arrest warrant," Jordan said. "I think we have enough now." He smiled at his team. "All we have to do is find them. I'll step up observations on their house, though I don't reckon they'll go back there. Not unless there is an overriding reason. Right, I'm going back in to speak with this matron. She's being far from open and honest, and this might be a bit of a lever. Keep up the good work, find me a car with them in it and you can go home early."

"Yeah, on it, boss. We're already canvassing car hire companies in Anglesey. By the way, it's past shift end." She was laughing as she hung up the phone.

When he went back into the matron's room, Jordan didn't address his comments to Rose Heath, but told Stella that the couple were in the country and that surely it was only a short time before they were found. It was an exaggeration of his confidence in the forthcoming arrest, but he wanted Rose Heath unsettled. He sat back in the chair and stared directly at the woman in front of him without speaking. Stella waited quietly beside him. The silence stretched for several minutes until the tension became unbearable for Rose.

"I had nothing to do with what happened to Mr Vance," she said eventually. "I wouldn't have anything to do with something like that. Why would I know anything about his murder? That wasn't me." She dashed away tears that had trickled onto her cheeks.

"Okay," Jordan said. "So, what is the deal with you and the Griffiths?"

"I don't think they had anything to do with it, either. They wouldn't. I just don't believe that."

"If you're all innocent of any wrongdoing, what were these calls about and why are you so hesitant to talk about it? Do you know why the Griffiths left their cruise?"

"I don't know about the cruise. The calls were business. That's all. It's just business." By now she had fought back the tears again, and they saw her get a second wind and try to take control of her nerves.

"I think we need to take this back to the station," Jordan said. "We need to conduct this interview more formally."

"Am I under arrest?"

"Why would you be under arrest?" Jordan said.

Rose frowned at him and then buzzed on her intercom to the clinic manager to say that she was stepping out for a while. "Do I need a solicitor?"

"That's up to you," Jordan said. "Do you think you need one?"

She picked up her mobile phone, dialled a number, and arranged for someone from one of the legal firms in the city to meet her at the station. This alone told them what they already suspected. Despite her denials, she thought there was trouble coming.

* * *

It was late by the time they settled into the interview room. Rose Heath was pale and drawn and Janice Booth, the young woman the solicitors had sent, put a reassuring hand on her arm as she was asked to identify herself for the recording.

Rose confirmed that she knew the Griffiths but would not answer when they asked, again, about the phone calls. It wasn't long before the 'no comment' responses began to wear thin. When the solicitor insisted on a break, they arranged for tea to be brought and Jordan and Stella went to the canteen, where the pickings were thin and the lasagna dried out and lukewarm.

"I don't know how we're going to shift her, boss," Stella said. "Not now she's got her lawyer involved. They were all voice calls. If only they'd sent some texts, it might have helped."

"I'm thinking maybe they'd already thought of that. We've got a tap on her phone now, haven't we?"

"Yes, but what are the chances of them calling just now when we need it? They'd have to use their own phones and they must know we're monitoring them."

"But Rose doesn't know that, does she?" Jordan said.

When they re-entered the interview suite, Jordan carried a file, which he laid on top of the desk without opening it. His primary gambit was to remind Rose Heath that she was being obstructive. He opened the file and ran a finger down the unseen page.

"Tilly," he murmured. "Brenda." He quietly relayed the address of the halfway-house flats, the outpatient clinic, and the address in Rodney Street as he showed the file to Stella. He shook his head and sighed.

"We are piecing things together, Ms Heath. Slowly, I'll admit, but it's making some sort of sense. It's not looking good. We're going to apply to keep you here until we have a chance to examine more of the evidence. You can help yourself by telling us now how much involvement you had and just what business it was that you alluded to earlier."

"I was away when Mr Vance was killed. I was in Europe, you know that," she said.

"Yes, but this is a complicated investigation, and we are busy tying things together and that doesn't answer the question, Ms Heath."

The solicitor asked to be shown what evidence they had of wrongdoing and told Rose that she hadn't yet been cautioned and could leave at any time. Jordan closed the file and laid his hands on top of it and stared across the table where the woman wouldn't meet his gaze.

When she began to speak, the legal representative reminded her it was better not to say anything, but the tension had become too much, and the matron had made her decision.

Chapter 53

"He has an import business, Fred Griffith. He's done it for years. It's where he makes his money."

"Yep, we know about that," Stella said.

"Well, that's all it was. Export and import. I did some work with him on the side. He was just checking on deliveries when he rang. That's all it was."

Jordan didn't speak. He shifted slightly in his chair, ran his hands through his hair and took a deep breath.

Rose glanced at him. "That's what it was, just deliveries," she said.

"So, why would you be so sneaky about it?" Stella said. "If that's all it was, you could have told us. We'll be able to see the invoices, bills of lading, whatever, and then it'll all be cleared up."

The matron glared at her. "I haven't got access to that stuff. The paperwork and what have you."

Jordan cleared his throat. "So, if I understand it, you were travelling to Europe to facilitate import and export of what? Bandages, sticking plasters, bottles of disinfectant?" His voice was loaded with disbelief. "This is on top of your very responsible position at the clinic. Your visits to the inpatient facility and the halfway house recovery unit. You went off acting as some sort of agent but have no paperwork relating to these exports."

The matron stared down at the table. She wrung her hands and glanced at the solicitor. "I need to speak in private."

The detectives left the two women and walked back to the incident room. Kath was still there speaking on the phone to car hire firms in Wales. She pursed her lips and shook her head. Jordan held up a coffee cup, and she nodded enthusiastically.

"You might as well call it a day, Kath," he said. "You look whacked."

"Just got two more firms to do," she replied with her hand over the phone. "Might as well finish them. If they are in a hire car, it'll be easy to catch them on the road with ANPR. Once they leave the car, they're in the wind, aren't they?"

"Could be, but we need to ring round hotels and guest houses as well. Chances are they are exhausted from the journey, and they can't be daft enough to come home. They have to know we're watching for them," Jordan said.

"I'll do that when I've finished with the cars."

"No, it's late. See if Vi can do that. She can work from home if she wants. No point anyone setting off for the wilds of Snowdonia on the off chance."

"Cool," Kath said. "You know Snowdon isn't on Anglesey, don't you, boss?"

"Yeah, 'course I do." He grinned at her, and she wasn't sure who was doing the teasing.

Jordan and Stella gulped some coffee and then headed back to the interview room where Rose Heath was red-eyed and distressed.

The solicitor opened the conversation by asking what the deal would be if her client gave them information relating to ongoing illegal activities concerning the missing couple.

"Depends how much information, what the activities are and whether it results in arrest and prosecution. But you already know that I'm not in a position to make that decision. I need more information, and then I'll feed it up the line," Jordan said.

"I need more time to confer with my client," Janice Booth said.

Jordan's phone beeped. He glanced at the screen to see a message from Sharon telling him that Brenda was conscious, still very poorly, but expected to make a full recovery.

Jordan lifted his head and stared at Rose Heath. "Brenda Baxter, I think you know her?"

The solicitor raised a hand. "My client will wait to have any further conversation until we have worked out just how that will benefit her."

"No, wait. What's wrong with Brenda?" the matron asked. "Is she okay?"

Chapter 54

Lights in the hospital ward were turned to night-time low and most of the patients were asleep. Sharon sat beside Brenda's bed, which was behind a curtain. The girl had her eyes closed, but when Jordan and Stella arrived, she looked at them.

"I'm sorry," she said.

Jordan pulled a chair up beside the bed and leaned forward. "What are you sorry for?"

"Running off and not telling you."

"Okay, but you can tell me why you did it now? You must have been scared."

Brenda nodded and coughed. Jordan filled a plastic cup with water and handed it to her. She sipped and wiped her chin where she had spilled some of the drink.

"You're going to be okay," Jordan said. "We'll try to help you. We can get you into a programme to help with your drug addiction."

"No, you don't need to. Anyway, I can't go back to that place. You can't send me there. I'll be okay. Perhaps I'll go and stay with me mam. I haven't used nothing. That wasn't what happened. It was like one minute I was walking down the street and I didn't feel right, but then I just was here. Some girls found me. I know Jez thought I was using, but I wasn't. It was just painkillers, and I think I took too many, but I was scared to tell anyone. After what happened to Tilly."

"Where's your mum?"

"She's in Yorkshire. She lives with a bloke. I don't like him, he's handsy, but it'll be better than that hostel."

"If you go off to Yorkshire, we won't be able to help you very much. You don't need to go anywhere you don't want to," Jordan said.

Brenda smiled weakly. "You're nice. I like you."

Jordan grinned at her and patted her hand. "I'm glad. Do you feel up to answering a couple of questions? If you get tired or worried, just say and we'll leave you alone."

Brenda closed her eyes and took a deep breath. She didn't wait for questions. "I'll just tell you all about it. You won't want to help me after that, but I'll tell you anyway."

She began the story by insisting she hadn't thought she was doing anything wrong. Other patients in the hostel had followed the same route, and it had been normalised.

"They told us that if we did what they asked, it would clear the debt."

"What debt?" Jordan asked.

"For being in the hostel. They gave us a bill. All the stuff was on there: food, heating, laundry, treatment. I thought it was free. I would never have gone if I'd known I'd have to pay. No way I could never, ever pay what they said. I was told it was a charity. That woman was at the court, and she said it would be all taken care of. I thought that because the judge said I had to have treatment, that's what it was."

Jordan didn't speak. There was no point telling her how difficult it was to get free residential treatment and that it would have been more likely that she would be offered outpatient care. He knew this was a pivotal moment. He glanced at Sharon and Stella, both of whom acknowledged his unspoken warning.

Brenda wiped away tears that slid down her cheeks and continued. She had been promised a large payment that would clear her debts and leave her with money to live on.

She sighed. "It would have been boss. I could have got a place. It would have set me up, and they promised it wouldn't do me no harm. I was scared, well, anyone would be, but I said yes."

In his mind, Jordan began to understand what it had all been about, but the idea was so vile, the concept so foul that he was sickened.

"What did you have to do?" he asked.

"So, I had to go to the flats first for a bit. That was to make sure I was clean and sober and for them to do some tests. That was okay. We had a laugh, and it was warm, and we had good stuff to eat. Tilly tried to get me to leave, but I didn't listen to her. I didn't believe her when she said I could leave. She was living in a grotty place and I thought she was hiding. I didn't know what she was really doing."

"What was that?"

"Well, she was trying to stop what they were doing. I see that now. She wasn't hiding because she was scared, it was so she could get evidence. She was getting loads of evidence so people would believe her, and she could stop it. She knew it was wrong. A mate of hers had died last year and she'd been trying since then to get enough to prove what was going on."

"What was it they had you doing?" Jordan asked.

"Don't you know? I thought you'd know. With what happened to Tilly, I just thought you'd know by now."

"We know you've had surgery recently. Is it to do with that?" Jordan said.

She nodded and swiped at her nose with a soggy tissue.

"They said I had to be careful, or I could be ill. Well, that was right, look at me."

"Who told you that?"

"The doctors and the nurses in Poland. They sent me home with pills and stuff and they said I should keep warm and rest. I couldn't do that. Where was I supposed to do that?"

She had assumed that there would be help and care for her once she arrived in Liverpool, but found nothing. No-one to meet her at the airport, no-one to tell her where to go, and so she sought out Tilly.

"What about the money?" Stella had leaned in towards the bed and taken hold of Brenda's hand. "I thought you said there would be money."

There had been no money. Tilly couldn't give her a place to sleep on a settee for more than a couple of nights but she did promise to go and see Mr Vance and tell him exactly what condition her friend was in and that she hadn't received any payment.

"She said he was helping her. He was supposed to be getting stuff together so's they could make it stop. She never came back. I was supposed to meet her, and she never came."

Now the girl was sobbing loudly, and a nurse appeared at the end of the bed, telling them they would have to leave if the patient was becoming upset.

Brenda shook her head and said that she was okay. She wanted to finish telling them.

There wasn't much more to say. Tilly had gone to the consulting rooms in Rodney Street, and that was all she knew. After that, the next she heard about her friend was that she was dead, murdered in Ormskirk.

Brenda was exhausted, her eyes were closing, her face pale and clammy-looking.

"We'll come back, maybe in the morning, if you're well enough," Jordan said.

"Do you think you can get my money? I mean, they owe me., don't they? They've got my kidney – well, someone has. They should give me my money."

Chapter 55

It was cold out on the street with a wind blowing up from the River Mersey. Friday night was Friday night though, and scantily dressed girls staggered down the streets on towering heels, giggling and screeching. Sharon, Jordan, and Stella stood in the vast hospital doorway for a minute. They had walked the corridors in silence, not sure how to start the conversation.

"Let's get back to the office," Jordan said. "I need to get my head around this. Jesus! As you say, Stel, 'can open, worms everywhere.'"

Stella grimaced. "I know. I'd like to think this information has helped, but right now, it seems that it's thrown everything we thought we knew out the window."

"Well, it hasn't. We just need to regroup. Could it be that whoever murdered Vance was a disgruntled patient, someone who had been forced to have the surgery and regretted it?"

"That would have been a valid thought, boss. But then Brenda said he was going to blow the whistle on it all, so it doesn't fly," Stella said. "Blimey, the lads are having a busy night."

They could hear the scream of sirens as cars whipped through the city streets and see the flash of blue on the buildings close by.

Sharon pulled out her phone. "Wonder what's occurring." She peered at the screen and then puffed out her cheeks. "Shit, hostage situation. Something's going on in Canning Street."

There was a moment of stunned silence, and then they started to run.

* * *

The street was taped off as they had expected. There were blue-and-white cars everywhere, and an ambulance. Jordan and his team flashed their warrant cards at the officer in front of the scene tape.

"Who's in charge?" Jordan asked.

"The DCI's in attendance, sir. He's down there." The bobby pointed to an area across the road from the Vances' house.

Jordan turned to the others and nodded. "Looks like things have just become even more complicated. Okay, no point in us all being here. Stella, can you go back to the station and have a word with the matron? Tell her we know about the organ removals. See what reaction there is. It's just not possible that she's not involved. Well, you know what to do. I shouldn't mention what's happening here, but it's possible the whole station is buzzing with it and she'll know already."

"What about me, boss?" Sharon asked.

"Stick with me for now. Let's see what's what."

DCI Adam Trent was in full uniform. Stubble on his chin and red-rimmed eyes suggested that he'd come in from home where he had already been settled for the night. Jordan shook his hand and waited.

"DI Carr," Trent said, "thought you'd better be in on this. Sorry to interrupt your Friday night with a call-out."

"I wasn't called out, sir. We were at the Royal interviewing a witness when we heard the cars and checked the report. Can you fill me in?"

The DCI nodded and straightened his shoulders. "There was a triple nine call from Carol Vance. She's in hiding in there." He pointed at the darkened house. "There's an intruder, and all she knows for sure is that Phoebe Vance screamed a couple of times and then went silent. She is sure there's someone downstairs and she heard a man's voice. That's about it at the moment. Poor woman's terrified. I believe she's in a wardrobe."

"What's the plan, sir?"

"Haven't got a bloody plan, Carr. I don't have enough information and the chief constable is already on my back. He's on his way in and, well… He's insisting we pull out all the stops; he knows these people. We need to set up a group. I'll be gold and be best off back in the office to co-ordinate things."

As he spoke, the delayed message calling Jordan to the scene landed in his phone.

"You need to be silver on this," Trent continued. "We're trying to get back in touch with Carol Vance. We've told her to text if she's frightened as she'll be overheard speaking on the phone, but as of now there's no response."

Jordan dialled the number he had for Phoebe Vance and though the call connected, and he heard the ring tone, nobody was surprised when there was no response. The DCI was pulling on his gloves and replacing his hat, and before Jordan had dialled the Vances' landline, he was already striding towards his waiting transport.

"Keep me informed, Carr, and get them out of there. I've requested a hostage negotiator to be on standby if that's what we need. First, we need to know just what's happened."

With that, he slid into the rear seat and was driven off with the integral blue lights clearing a path through the thickening crowd of onlookers and gathering press.

Jordan and Sharon watched him go.

"Boss," Sharon said, "what can I do?"

"Nothing right now," said Jordan. "Just help to keep this pandemonium controlled. If we've got a hostage situation, all this noise and palaver is the last thing we want."

"Are you going to send for the negotiator?"

"No. At least not until I have a clearer idea of just what I'm dealing with."

He pulled out his phone and opened Google Earth to zoom in on the layout of the street and the roads around it. He took a deep breath.

"Right, come with me; grab a couple of uniform bods. You need to cover both ends of the street at the back. I might need a boost to get over the wall, so pick someone with muscles."

In the event, the wheelie bin was enough. As Jordan pushed it nearer to the wall, he spotted a bag. It looked too good to be rubbish and he handed it to one of the officers to secure as evidence before he clambered up to the top of the wall, dropping into the garden.

Chapter 56

In St Anne Street, Stella asked the custody sergeant to rouse Rose Heath. He questioned whether it was essential so late at night. In the end she had her way, insisting that they had new information, and it was now more important than ever to find the Griffiths and the matron was their best bet to accomplish that. She hinted it could be connected with what was causing such a furore out in the Georgian Quarter.

As it turned out, the woman was far from sleep. She was sitting upright on the narrow bunk, staring at the wall. She was dishevelled and distressed and had obviously been crying for at least some of the time alone in the cell, leaving her eyes red and sore-looking.

"You can call your solicitor back if you wish," Stella told her, "but we need to have another chat. Brenda Baxter has regained consciousness, and I've had a natter with her."

"Is she alright?"

"She will be, I think. Of course, it would be a big help if we knew just what is wrong with her. You're a medical professional. You surely know that the more information we have, the better her chances are."

"My solicitor said I shouldn't talk before we've agreed on a deal."

"That's up to you, of course. I have to say, though, that if you help us now, help us help Brenda, it will look good and will be taken into account. So, what do you reckon? Will you come and talk to me, or do we have to wait for the solicitor to drag herself in? Friday night, plus there's a bit of chaos in the city, could be a while."

* * *

While they waited for a cup of decent coffee brought from the incident room and a piece of toast from the canteen, Stella took a call from Kath.

"What the hell, Kath, don't you ever sleep?" she said.

"You know what it's like, Stel. Once you get hooked on something, it comes between you and your zeds. Anyway, thing is, I've located the Griffiths. The boss was spot on. They were in a little bed-and-breakfast place in Wales. The landlady was less than chuffed when I called her. Understandable, I suppose. This was about half eleven, but she got all focused when I told her there would be a patrol with her in two shakes and to make sure she was safe until then. Most excitement she's had for yonks, I reckon. I bet she can't wait for her mates to get up so she can tell 'em. The car should be there by now. They were sending a detective to ask them, first of all, to come in voluntarily and hold the threat of illegal documentation and obstruction of the police as a persuader. I sent the landlady a picture, but of course him and her had checked in using a different name. Grigg apparently. Mr and Mrs Frank Grigg, it's deffo them, though. Hadn't changed their initials, which is pretty common in cases like this, isn't it?"

"They reckon so, yeah. Hey, well done, Kath."

"I don't know if you've checked the report from the forensic accountants. It came in late this afternoon."

"No, I saw it, but I reckoned it could wait. Was there something?"

"There was indeed. The charity was making sizeable donations to the clinic, which, as we know, funded the hostel and the flats."

"Okay. We sort of knew that, didn't we?"

"Yes. But the payments to the charity are from overseas, mostly traced back to clinics in Europe, and the clever accountancy sods have matched them as near as dammit with the timings on the spreadsheet."

"Fuck."

"Exactly. Laundering the proceeds of the organ sales through the bloody clinic. What a rat's nest."

"The boss is going to be dead pleased."

"Is he there?"

"No, have you not seen what's going on? He's only down in the middle of that mess in Canning Street. There's a real shitshow at the Vances'."

Back in the interview room, the matron had begun to regain her previous demeanour. Stella didn't waste any time letting her know the Griffiths had been traced and would be on their way back to Liverpool to face questions. She pointed out that time was short if Rose wanted to get her account in first and agree some sort of deal.

She then went on to outline what she had been told by Brenda and then simply asked the matron what she could tell them. Again, she reminded her that if she wanted to, they could call in the solicitor, but she had already seen the slump of the other woman's shoulders and that look in her tired eyes that said she had had enough and just wanted the nightmare to be over.

"We were doing a good thing," Rose said. "We were helping people." As she spoke, the woman nodded as if to confirm to herself that it was true.

This was the moment they had been working towards. Rose Heath had the answer to so many questions and now she was ready to talk.

For the next half an hour, Rose Heath explained the system whereby Frederick Griffith and his wife had effectively blackmailed the recovered addicts to donate kidneys illegally in payment for unexpected bills for treatment at the hostel. The patients were led to believe that treatment was free until they were ready to leave, clean and sober, and the costs were huge.

"Some people turned out to be too damaged by the abuse to their bodies; some could pay, with help from parents and so on. We just let them go. The ones that we were really working with…"

Stella tutted at the euphemism and the matron lowered her gaze and muttered a quiet acknowledgement.

"Anyway, the ones that we encouraged to be involved were the ones with no family. We gave them a place to go after the hostel."

There was a pause. Stella didn't speak. She was afraid that any interference at this stage might discourage the final admission.

"They agreed; they all agreed to do it. We didn't force them."

Again, Stella judged it best not to voice her thoughts. She didn't know whether the woman actually believed that she had been doing good or if she was just putting the best spin she could on what they had done.

"We took them to clinics abroad, and they had the operations. It didn't do them any harm, not really. They were usually okay. Then they came back to UK and went on with their lives. They had some money."

"Do you know what happened to them?"

"No. There was no need to keep tabs on them once they returned."

"So, you just washed your hands of these people. Did you not follow up with them, make sure they were okay?"

"No, a flight back was paid for and, like I just told you, they had money."

"Except they didn't, did they?"

"Of course they did. We paid them."

"Brenda Baxter didn't get any money."

"Oh, well, I don't know what happened with her. She should have done. That wasn't really my concern. I can't help you with that."

"You have no idea whether they were paid or not, have you?"

"I thought they were." The matron stared at the tabletop as she spoke, unable to look Stella in the eye.

Stella laid the hard copy of the spreadsheet between them. "These dates, are they the dates that the patients were flown out to be operated on?"

Rose looked at the printout for a while, and then she nodded. "I think so. Where did you get this from? Did Fred Griffith keep this record? That was a bit short-sighted of him."

"No, it's not his. We know he was calling you at the same times as these flights were scheduled. He was checking in with you, wasn't he?"

Rose nodded. "Sometimes I went with the patients just to make sure things went smoothly. We worried some of them might not go through with it. If it worked out that there were any coming back, I sometimes travelled with them to the UK. That wasn't often, though; mostly they came on their own."

"Okay. I will want you to make a full statement and we need names. We're going to have to trace these patients. We need to make sure they're alright. This record is the one that Roland Vance was keeping."

"Vance?"

"Yes, Mr Vance."

"No, that's not right."

"How do you mean?"

"Well, he didn't know anything about it. He had nothing to do with it."

Chapter 57

There was absolute mayhem in the street. How had this happened? He hadn't been followed. Why would anyone follow him? Nobody ever took any notice of him. He followed other people. That was the way it worked.

He thought of the girl. The shock when he saw her at the top of the fire escape and then the buzz he had got as she ran from the clinic with him behind her, deep in the shadows, the smell of blood still in his nostrils. The sticky feel of gore on his jacket and the thrill of the chase. He should have caught her then, but she was too quick for him. He'd known, though, he'd known where to go. Once a whore, always a whore, and he remembered her from the hostel and knew where she'd gone afterwards, so it had been easy to find her. Shame he'd had to throw the coat away, but some things just had to be done. Just like sitting outside her scuzzy shared house all night. It had worked out though. The next day, he had followed her on the train. Watching her scurrying away from him, scared and panicked, had been thrilling, like something out of a spy film. Then in the park. He remembered the feeling as his knife had flashed in the moonlight and she'd slumped onto the grass. A shudder passed through his body.

* * *

He looked down at the woman lying on the sofa sobbing. She gripped her throat, and blood seeped from between her fingers, running across the back of her hand to drip onto her jumper.

He could hear the cars, the sirens. It had all gone tits up and now he was stuck with this woman bleeding everywhere, police outside, and nowhere to go. How did they know? Somebody had told them.

"Who else is here, bitch?"

The woman raised her head to look at him. She was breathing oddly and having trouble keeping her eyes open. It didn't look good for her. It didn't look good for him. Maybe he should finish her now. Just off the old cow and then take whatever happened next. That's what a warrior would do.

"Nobody else," she croaked. "Just me. Why are you doing this?" She tried to shake her head, and more blood ran onto her chest. She gasped and groaned. "Help me, please, Phil. It is Phil, isn't it?"

"You shouldn't have struggled. You shouldn't have screamed. I wasn't going to cut you. I just wanted what you owe me."

"But I paid you."

"Not enough. I want more."

She shook her head. "There is no more. I gave you all I had. The police are outside. Just let them in. Get me an ambulance. It's over for you."

"It's over for you as well. If I go down, I'll take you with me. Though I don't think you'll last long. I'll tell them you took advantage. I'll tell them you forced me to kill the old bloke. You'll be dead, won't be able to argue."

"Me? They won't believe you. How could I force you to do anything?"

"I'll tell them about the hostel. What about that thug, Greg? They need to know about him, about how he bullied us. Poor me, a struggling sick patient. I'll say I was scared you would make them take me and about the people you sent to have operations, the ones that never came back."

"Of course they came back. Just because you never saw them doesn't mean they didn't come back. Look, you can get out of this."

He stared at her for a long minute and then waved his hand towards the window. "Oh yeah? How do you reckon that?"

"I'll tell them it was an accident. I'll say you were demonstrating that martial art, and you slipped."

"They'll never believe that. Why would they believe that?" To his horror, the idea of a possible escape brought tears to his eyes. He dashed them away and leaned in, bringing the blade close to her face. "Why would they believe that?"

"They'll believe me. I can convince them. I'm respected. I know important people. I'm known for my charity work, all the things I've done. I've raised money for the hostel, me and my friend Pauline, and Fred. How do you think we've paid for the flats, the good food you've eaten, the rooms? We've worked at it for years. We're busy people, business people. It's not easy, you have to think outside the box, and it saved lives, people got organs they needed. It could have gone on and on if it hadn't been for that stupid girl talking to my husband. We didn't take much for ourselves, just something to cover our expenses. We had to keep up appearances, look professional."

Phil leaned in close. "Why did you make me do it? I would never have done this if it hadn't been for you." He was screeching now; the panic had taken over. Tears and snot ran down his face and dripped from the end of his chin. "Why did you make me do it? It's all your fault."

"Because I had to. You were my only option. I'd seen you with that knife. I'd watched you at the flats, waving it around, practising your moves, and so I decided you could do what I needed. I chose you. I knew you needed money. Greg told me how tough you were. You should be flattered."

"What do you mean, you had to?"

"Because of all this." She raised a quivering hand to indicate the room. "Because he was going to leave me, and it would have ruined everything."

"What do you mean, ruined everything? You're rich."

"Money isn't everything. It's not about money. I've worked hard. I didn't used to matter but I've made us important. People listen when I speak. I sit on committees, but he was going to ruin it all."

"Why was he going? I don't believe any of this. You're old. People like you, you don't split up. You're lying. Bitch, bitch, bitch."

"He was gay. It was our big secret, but he was going to tell everyone. He said he couldn't live a lie any longer. Stupid, stupid man. It had worked for years, but now he was going to leave. I would be a laughing stock. People would pity me. We were supposed to be the perfect couple, special, but if I let him go everyone would know." She groaned and pushed to her feet. "I couldn't bear it. It was when he found out about the hostel, he said it was the final straw; all too much falsehood, too much lying. He said he had records. Everything was going to come out. It would all fall apart. You can see, it would ruin it all. Not just for me, for everyone, for all of us. He was going to spoil it all. Years it was just my secret; Roland called it my 'do-gooding'. He had no idea what we did, how we helped people."

She reached out and grabbed at him, staggering across the bloodstained carpet.

"Help me, please. Just get help." She raised her head, took in a breath as deep as she could and called out, "Carol." The effort was too much, and she slid to the floor, her hands streaking gore down the front of his clothes and she lay in a heap at his feet.

Chapter 58

Jordan was crouched in the shadows under the garden wall. There was a stretch of lawn edged with shrubs, and, near the house, a set of garden furniture sat on a flagged patio. The back of the building was in darkness. As far as he could see in the dimness, there was no sign of a break-in. Sticking close to the darkened borders, he stepped slowly towards the back door. The noise from the road was muffled but he could hear the beat of the helicopter rotors. The eye-in-the-sky lights swept over the scene. He cursed quietly. There was a thud from behind him and he turned to see Sharon pushing herself upright in the flower border and brushing damp soil from her jeans.

She shuffled nearer. "Sorry, boss, couldn't just wait out there," she hissed. "The back road's covered by coppers. I've had a message from Stel. I thought you should know, and I reckoned you'd have your phone on silent." She held out her phone so that he could read the message with the news that Vance was not involved with the hostel crime.

Jordan frowned and shook his head as he clicked off the screen and handed the phone back. "First things first. Let's sort this and then we can try to make sense of it all."

They knew there was a movement sensor, and it would likely be impossible to avoid the flood of light that would result once it was triggered. The aim was to avoid that as long as possible. He crouched low, shining the light from his phone downwards on the uneven ground. He wagged a hand towards Sharon, indicating that she should stay behind him and hug the dark spaces.

* * *

Back in the police station, Stella was struggling on her own. The matron was still insisting that Vance had not known about the organ sales and yet the spreadsheet said differently.

"I knew about Fred Griffith's phone," Rose said. "The one he used to call me. I sent somebody to get it back. But they couldn't find it. I just thought he must have taken it with him. Where was it?"

"I don't think that's important right now," Stella said.

"I suppose not. But I'm telling you, Roland knew nothing about the kidneys."

"Who tried to get it back for you?"

"It was a boy from the hostel. A bit of a weirdo. He'd already been in trouble for housebreaking. Anyway, he failed."

Stella showed her the picture of the person leaving the house in Allerton.

"Is this him?"

The matron glanced at the image and nodded. "Could be, yes."

Stella noted another problem solved, but they still had to find him. "Do you know where he is now?"

"He was at the flats for a while. I felt sorry for him. He's ill but I don't think he realises just how seriously. He was strange, into some sort of Japanese fighting of some kind. I don't know if he's still there. I haven't been in since I came back from my trip."

"What's his name?"

"Phil, Phil Swetenham, I think."

Stella made a note of the name and sent it through by text to Jordan and Sharon. Who knew what they were dealing with, but all information was useful.

Still, Rose insisted Tilly hadn't ever lived at the flats. The girl had refused to consider the kidney donation but had no family to pay her bill.

"The stupid thing ran away. One day she was there and then she wasn't," Rose said. "She was trouble right from the start. The other residents found her disturbing, and she was forever poking her nose into things that didn't concern her."

"Did you try to find her?"

"No. The chances were that she would be back on the drugs and drink. We had to have the patients closely monitored before the operations and once she'd gone, that wasn't possible. We had to just write her off. She wasn't important, just a thorn in my side."

"So, you didn't arrange to have her followed? It wasn't you and your mates who had the poor thing butchered?"

"No, no. What do you think we are?" The matron gasped.

Stella stared across the table until Rose Heath flushed and lowered her gaze.

"We wouldn't have done that. We wouldn't," she muttered.

The woman was sent back to her cell. Stella had repeated that she couldn't make any promises regarding a deal but that everything would be considered and as soon as it could be arranged, they would take her statement and get a time for her to appear in court.

Now Stella was staring at the whiteboard. She wanted to be with Jordan, who she knew could be in danger, but there was nothing she would be able to do out in the dark, damp streets along with all the other officers just waiting for things to happen. They were managing to keep the press under control and coverage on the news was minimal, but that would no doubt change with the dawn, when they would need to inform commuters and shoppers about road closures and diversions.

She tried to call Jordan and Sharon, but both phones went straight to voicemail. Contacting the control room told her very little, except that the incident was ongoing.

Everyone who was available had been sent to the Georgian Quarter. With a shrug, she walked out into the drizzle and the cold wind. She had her ASP in her hand as she headed along St Anne Street. There were blue-and-white cars evident in the area and the air support circling. She could drive, but the place was no doubt awash with vehicles already and the walk might help to get her thoughts in order.

* * *

Jordan and Sharon had made it more than halfway through the garden before the security light flashed on. As it did, they pressed back against the wall and froze. After a while, they were again plunged into darkness.

When their eyes had readjusted to the gloom, they peered at the back windows, waiting to see if someone would come to investigate. There was no movement visible in the shadowy kitchen. No torchlight, no sudden illumination in the room.

"We'll make a run for it. If we can get on the other side of the patio and close to the back door, the light will come on, but it'll go out again," Jordan said, "probably."

He tensed and took in a breath. "The chances of that door being open are slim, but I don't see any other option right now but to go for it, fast as you can."

Sharon nodded and grunted.

As they expected, the sensor picked them up when they ran across the paving, but once close to the back door, they waited and after what seemed like hours, it clicked off. Jordan reached out and pushed down the handle. The door opened, and he turned to raise his eyebrows at Sharon as they crept quietly into the kitchen. In the dim borrowed light from the hallway, they could see that it was clean and tidy, but the tiles were marked with dark smears, and there were streaks and spots of blood on the door frame leading into the hallway.

They stood in the kitchen, ears straining for any noise. The sound of quiet muttering could be heard from the direction of the living room.

There was a creak and a hiss from the staircase. They looked up to see the terrified face of Carol Vance peering from behind the banister. Jordan lifted a finger to his lips. She pointed towards the living room.

Chapter 59

The sobbing had stopped, but now there were other sounds from behind the blood-streaked door in the hall.

Carol descended another step and wagged her hands, urging them to move. Jordan nodded. The woman was scared out of her wits and she lowered herself carefully to sit on the stairs. The blood was worrying and Jordan leaned forward, listening for a hint of what might be happening just out of sight. There were thuds and grunts, and it was impossible to imagine just who was doing what, and then he heard the quiet voice.

There was a hint of hysteria, turning the words into a whispered hiss. "You're going to die. You're going to bleed out if you don't get help."

The crying began again.

"No good snivelling, but listen, I'm going to help you. Yes, I am. That detective, the black guy, the one that's been hanging round. Have you got his number?"

There was a mumbled response.

"Give me your phone."

Jordan dragged his own mobile from his pocket.

The device was already on silent. He turned to Sharon and pointed up the stairs to where Carol was crouched, shivering on the step. Sharon nodded and scurried across the carpet and up to the distressed woman. She pulled her to her feet and ushered her up and into the nearest bedroom.

Jordan retreated to the kitchen and out into the cold garden before the light on his screen indicated a call from Phoebe Vance.

He swept his finger across the screen to answer the call.

"Carr. Who is this?"

"Never mind who it is. I've got Mrs Vance here. She's hurt, badly. She's dying."

Jordan heard a cry of despair. "Let me come in. I'm just outside."

"No way. You and all your mates. No. I want something in return."

"We can talk about that. Just let me come in and help Mrs Vance and then we'll sort all this out. Is this Phil?"

"Never you mind, it doesn't matter. I want out. I want a car. Not a police car, something like a taxi."

"A taxi? I can't do that."

"Well, you'll have to. I can't drive and I'm not going in no cop car, I'm not stupid. You'll have to be quick. She's not got long. Once the taxi arrives, I'll let you help her. Get me one of them Ubers."

Jordan wondered just what the reaction would be if he called an Uber for a murderer.

"That's just not possible. You must see that. Look, let's just talk. How about I come into the house, and we see what's what? But there's just no way you're getting an Uber."

"She's going to die then."

"That won't help you though, will it? Think about it. Once she's dead, we'll just come in there and take you down. There would be nothing to lose."

There was silence except for the whimpering in the background. It was impossible to know how badly hurt the woman was, but obviously, they needed to act quickly.

"How about I just let you out, Phil? I'll let you out of there. Tell the troops to hold back and let you leave." He wouldn't believe that, would he? Then again, he had just asked for an Uber.

"You'll make sure they don't grab me?"

"Yeah. I'll tell them all to stand down."

"Nah. You must think my head zips up the back. I'm not stupid."

"Said the man who just asked the police to get him an Uber," Jordan said. "You're out of your depth. There's no way back from this. Either she dies and we come in and you're done for murder, or you let us in now and we help her, and it gets taken into account and things go easier for you."

Another silence. This was ridiculous. It couldn't go on. They were running out of time.

Jordan had never done a negotiators course; he wasn't a psychologist. All he had was instinct, the element of surprise if he went now, and maybe some luck.

He didn't hang up on the phone call, no point telegraphing his intentions. Once he had laid it quietly on the paving, he picked up a large stone ornament, something abstract with smooth edges. He hefted it and turned it to get the best grip.

He took a deep breath, sent a wish to Nana Gloria, who always looked out for him, and went back into the house, through the kitchen, down the hallway and, pausing for just a moment, he stormed into the living room.

The first thing he noticed was the blood everywhere and a semi-conscious woman, lying on the couch with her hand clasped around her throat.

Standing in front of her was a tall, thin youth. He was dressed in loose black trousers and a short jacket with a badge on one side. In his hand was a large, evil-looking knife, smeared in blood. As the youth turned to look at the figure crossing the floor, he raised the weapon with two hands in front of his chest, planted his feet apart and bent his knees. He waved the blade back and forth in an arc in front of him and a slow grin spread across his face.

Jordan stopped, watching the strange mash-up of contact sport, kung fu films, anime, and graphic novels. On the settee, Phoebe Vance had lost consciousness. Through the window the sweep of blue light from the emergency vehicles created patterns on the walls.

"Okay," Jordan said, "enough. Stop arsing around, just put the knife on the floor, Phil. Kick it towards me. Do it now."

The thug raised his chin and snorted and let go a shout. He was lost in his own world, a hero fighting for his freedom.

Jordan moved forward, holding the garden ornament in front of him with both hands. The zombie knife looked heavy, tough, and very sharp. If it made contact, it would be bad, really bad. Jordan's Nana Gloria and his mum had brought up a brood of children, keeping them safe and turning them into decent, successful adults. They had been bullied because they wore their school uniforms and avoided the gangs. He had protected his younger brothers from street thugs. This wasn't new to him, and the only way to deal with it was to take control. Delay was dangerous and to back off was unthinkable.

With a blood-curdling yell, he launched himself across the floor, the lump of concrete raised above his head, and he brought it down with all the power in his shoulders onto the hands holding the knife.

The youth screamed and spun around as the weapon flew from his grip. He stared down at his damaged hands and groaned. The knife was an arm's length away, but with no control over his fingers, it was a lost cause. He threw himself to the floor to try and reach for his weapon. Jordan rushed forward, intent on kicking the knife to safety. Wriggling across the carpet, Phil stretched towards the ornate handle and tried desperately to pull it nearer with his bleeding, twisted digits. His fingers were useless and he couldn't grip the weapon.

Jordan came closer. He placed the garden ornament on the floor and pulled the speed cuffs from his pocket. Phil screeched and rolled away. He struggled to his feet and threw himself at Jordan, smashing against his legs. The big detective was thrown off balance and fell, landing on top of the groaning youth. Phil opened his mouth and bit down hard on Jordan's neck, tearing at the flesh, shaking his head. A dog gone mad. Jordan yelled out in pain.

Sharon leapt in from the doorway, picked up the concrete statue and smashed it down on the upper body of the younger man. Phil screamed again as his shoulder popped out of the joint and one arm bent at an unlikely angle. He looked down at his battered body. His eyes rolled back in his head, and he slumped unconscious at Sharon's feet.

Jordan was holding onto the side of his neck and scrabbling in his pocket for a handkerchief. Holding the cloth as a pad against the bleeding and with a grimace of pain, he took a couple of steps, leaned and pressed his fingertips to the neck of the kidnapper. There was a pulse. He hoped they hadn't done irreparable damage to his arms, but there had been no other option. He borrowed Sharon's phone, and as he felt the thready, weak beat in the neck of Phoebe Vance, he speed-dialled Stella. She would be there; he had no doubt at all.

"Come in now, paramedics and uniforms. I've got injuries."

"Boss, are you okay?"

"Yeah, but other people aren't. Come on in, Stel."

Chapter 60

The first ambulance took Phoebe Vance. The paramedics had started infusions to replace some of the fluid lost, but a blood transfusion was required urgently. A large dressing covered the wound on her neck. Carol Vance rode in the ambulance with her sister-in-law. She was wrapped in a silver survival blanket, shocked and bewildered but not physically injured.

A second ambulance screamed along the street and the medics began the slow process of loading Phil onto a backboard, a cervical collar around his neck, oxygen mask, and tubes carrying painkillers and fluids. He hadn't regained consciousness and as Jordan moved aside to let them pass with the gurney, he felt sick to think that he had been responsible for most of the harm. Sharon was on the settee, her face pale, and her hands quivering. She tried to hide them by crossing her arms to hug herself.

"You did good, Sharon. Thank you," Jordan said.

"Bloody hell, boss. I heard the bones go. I smashed his arms, and did you see his shoulder?"

"I'd already done a lot of the damage. There wasn't anything else you could do, really. You stopped him and prevented him doing much more than this to my neck. You did what you had to do. Don't beat yourself up about this."

"How is it, your neck?"

Jordan grimaced and raised a finger to gently touch the dressing. "Bloody hurts, to be honest. The paramedics cleaned it up and stuck some stitches on it but I'll have to follow up and have tetanus injections and–" He stopped. "We have to have him checked for Aids and hepatitis."

"Shit, boss!" She lifted a hand to lay it on his arm and, at the last moment, drew it back and stroked her hair awkwardly.

"Yeah. Not what I would have hoped for. It'll be fine. I'm sure it'll be fine. I'll get it seen to as soon as I can." He dredged up a wobbly smile.

They were exhausted and haggard from lack of sleep, but hyped up on adrenalin.

"Breakfast?" Stella said.

Jordan rubbed his eyes. "I don't think I'm up for it, to be honest. Let's get back, see if the on-duty nurse can give me the tetanus shot. I can't face the A&E right now."

* * *

In the end they couldn't be bothered to find a café and weren't in the mood for company, so they trudged in silence through the wakening city. Kath and Vi were already in the incident room. The coffee was hot and fresh and they had picked up pastries and sausage rolls on the way in. Jordan's neck throbbed and his head pounded. The thought of the paperwork was vile, and he needed to ring Penny, who would be out of her mind with worry. He always tried to let her know what was happening, but this time there had been no chance.

"Just going to call Penny," he told the others.

"I sent her a message earlier," Stella said. "Just told her you were okay."

"Thanks, mate. Appreciate that. Still, I'll speak to her." He glanced at his watch. It was very early, but Harry would be awake, and he doubted his wife would've had slept much. He walked into his office and threw himself into the desk chair.

Kath appeared at the door. "Sorry, boss. The Griffiths have arrived. We've got them downstairs. They're in separate rooms, but given they came back in one car, it's pointless really. They'll already have conferred about whatever story they're going to give us. Do you want me to speak to them?"

The temptation to hand it over was huge. After all, they surely knew all there was to know, and this was just tidying up the facts. He blew out a big breath. "No, it's great. Thanks. Will you sit in? I'll be just a few minutes."

Pauline Griffith didn't look well. She was already sobbing when Jordan and Kath went into the interview room and started the recording.

"Do you want a solicitor?" Jordan asked.

They didn't tell her that her husband had already demanded his solicitor be sent for and was currently sat in the cell, sullen and angry while he waited.

In the end, it was easier than they had anticipated. Even Frederick Griffith admitted everything once his solicitor had a word. The blackmail and bullying of recovering addicts, the illicit sale of body parts, and he even admitted to the tax fraud that the forensic accountants had discovered as they worked their way through his accounts.

He was furious when they told him that Rose Heath had already given them everything they needed to submit to the CPS, leaving him with nothing to offer to make a deal. His angry bluster was just that and soon blew itself out.

The nurse gave Jordan his injection and dressed the bite on his neck. When he thought of the other issues, his stomach roiled. Aids, hepatitis. It was terrifying.

Back in his own office, he popped a couple of painkillers and wondered how to tell Penny about the repercussions of what had happened and the fear he was struggling with.

Stella knocked on the door and leaned into the space. "Quick word, boss?"

"Okay, then get off home. You look like death warmed up."

"Ha, pot and kettle, boss. You need to go as well. The others can start the paperwork. But I just want to let you know. I had a word with Charlotte Burley."

"Erm, the nurse?"

"Yeah. She did me a solid. That bloke, the one who bit you. Well, he was a patient, yeah."

"Yes, of course."

"So, he's already had all the checks they need to have. Like they told us, he's not well, so they've been monitoring him. I guess that, even with everything else, there were decent medics attached to the clinic who just did their jobs. It's a shame we're going to have to investigate all of them. Anyway–" She paused and just looked at him. "Well, that means they already know all about his health."

"Oh." He waited, his heart thudding, scared to ask, trying to read her face.

She grinned at him. "God, your face. It's okay, boss. He hasn't got anything horrible. Well, he has but nothing that you need to worry about. She can't put it in writing or nothing. Patient confidentiality and that, but she said to tell you not to worry. The results when they come back will be fine."

Jordan let go the breath he didn't realise he'd been holding. He couldn't speak, and Stella just looked at him. She walked into his office and around the desk to wrap her arms around him in a warm hug. Stepping back, she glanced at the open door to make sure she hadn't been seen. She rubbed a hand across her face and cleared her throat, then nodded and turned to leave.

"Probably no need to bother Penny with that crap then, eh? You off home now?"

Jordan frowned as he straightened the paperwork on his desk. Then he raised his head and looked her in the eye. "I am, but I just thought I'd call in and see Brenda, let her know we've sorted it all and we'll see what we can do about finding her somewhere to stay. Do you want to come?"

"Nah. I'm done being the bearer of good news. Too much pink and fluffy'll make me nauseous. Tell her I hope she gets better soon." Stella left the office and marched across the room and into the toilet where she stood for a while, running cold water across her hands.

* * *

At the hospital, the girl was sitting in a chair looking out at the busy main road. "Have you decided what you want to do?" Jordan asked.

"Not really. I'll go to my mam's and take it from there. But I'm staying off the drugs. I'm done with all that. This has been a real wake-up call for me."

She insisted on giving Jordan a kiss on his cheek before he left, and he was walking down the corridor with a smile on his face when he saw a familiar figure in front of him.

"John. What are you doing here, at this time of the morning? How's your dad?"

There was no need to wait for a response. The DC raised a hand holding a white plastic bag. "His stuff."

"Oh, mate, I'm sorry. What happened?"

John shook his head, unable to speak, and Jordan reached out to lay a hand on his shoulder. "I'll let them know at the office. Don't worry. Take your time. I'll inform HR and all of that."

"Thanks, boss. Oh, I heard about the case. Good result, eh?"

"It was, and we couldn't have done it without you and your work on that spreadsheet."

"Yeah, you would. Someone would have done it. But thanks."

There was just one more job before he went home, and Jordan followed the signs to the ICU where Phil Swetenham was in a bed behind a curtain with a PC sitting on a hard chair alongside. He had regained consciousness but he was on heavy-duty painkillers and unaware of anything going on around him. One arm was heavily bandaged, and his neck was still covered with a collar and black bruises crept out from underneath.

As Jordan stood looking down at him, a young doctor with a clipboard came to stand beside him. "Are you a relative?"

"Nope." Jordan took out his warrant card.

"Oh, right. I need some information, but I don't think you'll be able to give it to me. I need to start the process of putting him on the list."

"List?"

"Yeah. Transplant. He's in need of a new kidney and as soon as possible. We're going to start dialysis, but that's only a temporary measure."

"You know what he's done? He's going to be tried for two particularly nasty murders and a wounding and that's just the start. He's going away for a long time."

The doctor looked Jordan in the eye. "Not my problem. He needs a new kidney, end of. He might be lucky, but they are hard to get. We'll see."

With that, he walked away and left Jordan standing in the middle of the ward, aching and exhausted.

He looked down at the skinny youth under the sheets, shook his head, and turned to walk out of the hospital and go home to his wife.

The End

List of characters

Detective Inspector Jordan Carr – Jamaican heritage. Married to Penny. They have one little boy, called Harry. Lives in Crosby. Drives a VW Golf.

Detective Sergeant Stella May – Liverpool, born and bred. Lives in Aintree. Drives an electric VW ID5.

Detective Constable John Grice – Regular part of Jordan's team. A Scouser who lives in Old Skelmersdale.

DCI Josh Lewis – Detective Chief Inspector in charge at Copy Lane.

DC Kath Webster – Junior officer.

DC Violet Purcell – Junior officer. Has spent all her working life in the force and is retiring in a couple of years. Three children, happily married.

PC Sharon Taylor – Ambitious young constable. Tall and dark-haired. Lives in Kirkby.

Ted Bliss – Crime scene sergeant. Sarcastic and funny but also sympathetic.

Dr James Jasper – Medical examiner based at the University of Liverpool and Liverpool Central Morgue. Very grumpy and short-tempered.

Dr Phyllis Grant – Medical examiner. Locum for when Jasper is unavailable.

Vickie Frost – SOCO sergeant.

DS Jane Keene – Detective from West Lancashire, brought in as liaison regarding one of the murders.

DCI Adam Trent – St Anne Street murder squad.

Roland Vance – Consultant surgeon.

Phoebe Vance – Roland's wife.

Carol Vance – Roland's sister.

Charlotte Burley – Senior clinic nurse.

Rose Heath – Clinic matron.

Vivienne Campbell – Clinic manager.

Gilly Gudgeon – The Vances' cleaner.

Pauline Griffith – Patient.

Frederick Griffith – Pauline's husband.

Tilly Mount – Patient.

Brenda Baxter – Patient.

Jez – Squatter.

Greg – Manager at rehab hostel.

Gordon Warner – Caretaker at the flats.

If you enjoyed this book, please let others know by leaving a quick review on Amazon. Also, if you spot anything untoward in the paperback, get in touch. We strive for the best quality and appreciate reader feedback.

feedback@joffebooks.com

www.thebookfolks.com

Also by Diane M. Dickson

DETECTIVE JORDAN CARR
Book 1: BODY ON THE SHORE
Book 2: BODY BY THE DOCKS
Book 3: BODY OUT OF PLACE
Book 4: BODY IN THE SQUAT
Book 5: BODY IN THE CANAL
Book 6: BODY ON THE ESTATE
Book 7: BODY BELOW THE BRIDGE
Book 8: BODY IN THE WAY

DI TANYA MILLER INVESTIGATES
Book 1: BROKEN ANGEL
Book 2: BURNING GREED
Book 3: BRUTAL PURSUIT
Book 4: BRAZEN ESCAPE
Book 5: BLURRED LINES

THE YORKSHIRE CRIME MYSTERIES
Book 1: TWIST OF TRUTH
Book 2: TANGLED TRUTH

STANDALONES
LEAVING GEORGE
WHO FOLLOWS
LAYERS OF LIES
PICTURES OF YOU
YOU'RE DEAD
THE GRAVE
DEPTHS OF DECEPTION
SINGLE TO EDINBURGH
BONE BABY
HOPELESS

DISCOVER MORE BOOKS BY DIANE DICKSON

DETECTIVE JORDAN CARR
BOOKS 1–8 BOX SET

Eight crime novels packed with twists, strong characters, and authentic British policing, all in one super-value box set!

DI Jordan Carr is still settling into his new role when a woman's body is found on the beach at Crosby. But it's only the beginning. Over eight challenging investigations, Carr must lead a stretched team through a series of chilling cases: a missing woman, a corpse in someone else's grave, a killing in a derelict squat, and a murder with only a "psychic" old woman for a witness. Set in Liverpool and across Merseyside, these are tense, tightly plotted police procedurals that don't flinch from the realities of modern policing.

Out now on Amazon!

BROKEN ANGEL

Book 1 in the DI Tanya Miller Investigates series

An eerie corpse dressed as a bride, a killer playing a macabre game, and a woman detective prepared to follow her instincts. Enter DI Tanya Miller, the missing persons specialist brought in to investigate the disappearance of a woman from a motorway services. Someone is playing a sick game, and she's determined to catch them, no matter what it takes.

Out now on Amazon!

THE BOOK FOLKS

Thank you for choosing this book.
Join our mailing list and get FREE Kindle books
from our bestselling authors every week!

www.joffebooks.com/freebooks

www.ingramcontent.com/pod-product-compliance
Ingram Content Group UK Ltd.
Pitfield, Milton Keynes, MK11 3LW, UK
UKHW020840190825
7464UKWH00025B/167